HARRIET SAID

HARRIET
SAID

BERYL BAINBRIDGE

GEORGE BRAZILLER

NEW YORK

Published in the United States in 1973 by George Braziller, Inc.
Copyright © 1972 by Beryl Bainbridge
Originally published in England by Gerald Duckworth & Co. Ltd.

Standard Book Number: 0–8076–0687–1
Library of Congress Catalog Number: 73–76970
Printed in the United States of America
First Printing

For Lord Roland

HARRIET SAID

1

ARRIET said: 'No you don't, you keep walking.' I wanted
to turn round and look back at the dark house but she
tugged at my arm fiercely. We walked over the field hand in
hand as if we were little girls.

I didn't know what the time was, how late we might be. I
only knew that this once it didn't really matter. Before we
reached the road Harriet stopped. I could feel her breath on
my face, and over her shoulder I could see the street lamps
shining and the little houses all sleeping. She brought her
hand up and I thought she was going to hit me but she only
touched my cheek with her fingers. She said, 'Don't cry
now.'

'I don't want to cry now.'

'Wait till we get home.'

The word home made my heart feel painful, it was so lost
a place. I said, 'Dad will have got my train ticket back to
school when I get in. It will be on the hall table.'

'Or behind the clock,' said Harriet.

'He only buys a single. I suppose it's cheaper.'

'And you might lose the other half.'

'Yes,' I said.

We stood for a moment looking at each other and I won-
dered if she might kiss me. She never had, not in all the years
I had loved her. She said, 'Trust me, I do know what's best.
It was all his fault. We are not to blame.'

'I do trust you.'

'Right. No sense standing here. When I say run, you start

to run. When I say scream, you scream. Don't stop running, just you keep going.'

'Yes,' I said, 'I'll do that, if that's what's best.'

'Run,' said Harriet.

So we ran over the last stretch of field and Harriet didn't tell me to scream, at least I didn't hear her, because she was really screaming, terrible long drawn out sounds that pierced the darkness, running far ahead of me, tumbling on to the road and under the first street lamp, her two plaits flying outwards and catching the light. I hadn't any breath to scream with her. I was just wanting to catch up with her and tell her not to make that noise. Somebody came out of a house as I went past and called to me but I did not dare stop. If I couldn't scream for her then I could run for her. A dog was barking. Then we were round the bend of the lane and there were lights coming on in the houses and my mother on the porch of our house with her fist to her mouth. Then I could scream. Over her head the wire basket hung, full of blue flowers, not showing any colour in the night.

I did notice, even in the circumstances, how oddly people behaved. My mother kept us all in the kitchen, even Harriet's parents when they arrived, which was unlike her. Visitors only ever saw the front room. And Harriet's father hadn't got a collar to his striped shirt, only a little white stud. Harriet could not speak. Her mother held her in her arms and she was trembling. I had to tell them what had happened. Then Harriet suddenly found her voice and shouted very loudly, 'I'm frightened,' and she was. I looked at her face all streaked with tears and I thought, poor little Harriet, you're frightened. My father and her father went into the other room to phone the police. My mother kept asking me if I was sure, was I sure it was Mr Biggs.

Of course I was sure. After all I had known him for years.

* * *

2

When I came home for the holidays, Harriet was away with her family in Wales. She had written to explain it was not her fault and that when she came back we would have a lovely time. She said that Mr Redman had died and that she had spoken to him only a few days previously. He had inquired what she was going to do when she left school. She said she might go on the buses. 'Likely you'll get more than your ticket punched,' he had replied. It was a nice farewell thing to say. Harriet said we should bow the head at the passing of landmarks.

His was one of the earliest faces Harriet and I remembered patrolling the lane down to the sea; in company with the Tsar, Canon Dawson from St Luke's and Dodie from Bumpy field.

Mr Redman, to be specific, never went into the lane. In winter he stayed in his bungalow and waved from the window, in summer he bent down to his garden. We talked to him a little, either over his hedge or his gate, about his nice flowers or his nasty weeds.

The Canon rode a bicycle, a big one with two back wheels and no crossbar. Typical, as Harriet said, seeing he was such a Child.

Dodie always walked down the lane, swollen ankles in apricot stockings, dressed forever in black. She would cry out to us as she passed our fence, 'Hallo Pets . . . How's my Pets?' She lived in a bungalow next to the lunatic asylum, handy for Papa, her husband, as Harriet said.

The Tsar had been walking down to the sea the first evening

that Harriet and I had gone to collect tadpoles from the ponds below the pine trees. Slightly unsober, slightly dishevelled, always elegant, he swayed moodily past us through all the days of our growing up. We acknowledged him briefly, as indeed we acknowledged the Canon whom we detested, and Mr Redman and darling Dodie. But it was only twice he spoke to us: once to admire our captured tadpoles that he said were like prehistoric embryos, and another more memorable time when looking away from us toward the sea, he had said,

'Years ago I visited Greece . . . beautiful beyond compare.'

Harriet, watching his face and perceptive to his mood, had cried, 'What were the statues like, all those lovely statues?'

It was then the Tsar looked at me, not a shadow of doubt, though it was her he answered.

'Scarred beauties, Harriet, chipped no end. Figures with noble noses and robust limbs, but beautiful.'

Harriet stood on one leg when he had gone, pointing her finger and hopping in a circle round me. 'He thinks your nose noble,' she sang, 'noble and robust, but beautiful, my dear, so beautiful.'

I said I did not care to be compared to Grecian ruins, then ran away among the trees, delighted with myself.

Later Harriet said his name was Peter Biggs and we should call him Peter the Great. But I thought the name Peter was daft so we called him the Tsar.

Without Harriet I was irritable and bored. I did not have any other friends, partly from inclination and partly because none of the families I knew sent their children to boarding school. I was a special case, as Harriet observed. I had gone when younger to a private school in the district, but I was a disgrace owing to the dirty stories found written in my notebook, and everyone agreed I was out of control and going wrong and in need of supervision. I did know, even without Harriet to tell me, that I had learned the shameful stories at school in the first place, that I did not have an original idea on the subject and that really they were scared of me and Harriet being so intimate. We were too difficult. Nothing else.

So I was sent to boarding school and heard new dirty jokes which I learnt by heart instead of committing them to paper. After a time I did not mind being away from home but it was a dreadful waste of money and my parents were not rich, not even wealthy. However I did speak nicely and I had a certain style.

The third morning I was home my father offered to drive me in his car to see the grave of Mr Redman. He was being kindly, but Harriet always said it was an insult the way he bought black-market petrol when other people suffered deprivations. However, she was not there to observe me.

When I entered the graveyard of the small Norman church there was the Tsar, head inclined a little to one side as I approached. A gentle breeze blowing from the pines lifted the thin hair on his head as he turned to greet me. My father sat in the car in the road and watched us shake hands in the sunlight.

'Ah, my dear child . . . Harriet said you were due home.'

'Why hasn't Mr Redman got a head stone?'

'It's expensive, you know.'

'More like no one's bothered.'

'Quite.'

Later, returning to the house, my father drove angrily, curving the car viciously round corners, asking, 'What did you say to him, eh? What did you find to say to the blighter?'

'Only that I had not seen him for years.'

'He's a scoundrel. Nothing but a damned scoundrel.'

He hunched his back in wrath over the wheel. He thought most people were scoundrels for one reason or another, mostly that I knew them. Burying my face in the warm leather seating I murmured to myself, 'A damned scoundrelly Tsar,' and thought complacently how fine it sounded.

That evening after my tea I went out in the rain to walk to the pines. There were two ways to the sea. One was straight down the lane past Harriet's bungalow on the left and the Tsar's house on the right, over the railway crossing and on to the cinder path leading directly to the pines with the ditch to cross. Once there had been a stream, but now it was just a cut in the ground, choked high with weeds and grasses.

Or you could go by the park bordered by privet, very neat with its clock-golf course and bowling green, two hard tennis courts, a wooden pavilion with thatched roof, and up the hill to the station. That was nice because there were railings and you could drag a stick across them all the way down the other side of the hill until you came to the Sunday school hut made out of tin with a bell on the roof; some ponies in the fields to the left, the Barracks away to the right and a single line of pines turning a corner of the road to the church fence.

It was a longer route but a good one.

I climbed over the stone wall, crossed the graveyard and went through the gate into the woods. I sang as I began to climb the slope among the trees, 'All through the night there's a little brown bird singing, singing in the hush of the darkness and the dew . . .' It was practically the only song I knew all through and it had the right note of melancholy suitable to a summer evening. The ground was nut brown with needles, but further along the sand had blown up from the dunes over the years and slid along the rise, a second sea, seeping in a white pool amongst the second row of trees. There were potholes in the earth left by the soldiers training there during the war. Once by mistake the Germans dropped a bomb, but the sand soon filled up the crater. On the other side of the road the woods covered the ground from the railway crossing to the beach. Here, at the end of the ridge, the ground dropped abruptly away to a flat hollow of grass and water. Behind that another rise of trees and then the dunes, half a mile of them, undulating up and down till they pushed the shore and the flat edge of sea.

I rolled all the way down the slope and reached the bottom covered with sand, breathless, not from exertion but because the Tsar was sitting by the tadpole ponds with his back to me. I was shy.

The ponds were no more than long puddles of rain-water set in the grass. In winter the rain fell endlessly, the pools thickened, mud formed. When the frost came, the ground hardened, the edges of the pools shrank, the ice pinched closer; the low bushes snapped at a touch, the tall dune grasses froze in clumps. Once, in the centre of the largest pool, Harriet and I saw two frogs, dead, bloated with water, floating, white bellies upward, like pieces of bread. Now in summer the water was warm to the touch. I crouched down in the sand and trailed my fingers back and forth waiting for him to speak first.

'Aah,' he said, letting out a sigh, as he lay back with his head in the grass, his trilby hat, which he never wore, beside him, its brim dipping in the water.

I said, 'Look there's a swallow,' as a bird plunged down to his hat and rose on the instant to fly upwards and away into the trees.

He, lazily turning his head, replied, 'Nonsense, girl, more likely a sand martin,' and lay back again.

I could not argue with him because, though I spent a great deal of time in the woods and considered myself a naturalist, I never truly knew one bird from another. Harriet with passion collected ferns and leaves and wrote down migration months in her scrap book, referring to flowers by dear latinic names, but I never remembered.

'What's your school like?' he said, 'not too bad?'

'Not bad. I've got used to it.'

'Being away from your parents will do you a power of good in the end. Develops your sense of identity.'

'It's jolly expensive.'

'Quite.'

He asked how long were the holidays and spoke conventional platitudes about my missing Harriet, and the mischief we would get up to on her return. I said, Yes, I did miss her, and Yes, no doubt we would get up to one or two larks. I was filled with distaste as I spoke; not at my sentiments but at the restraint that made me couch them so childishly. While I talked uneasily I watched the bird's skull of his head nestle a space for itself in the sand. The time might come I felt when I would be moved to stretch out a hand and cradle his head against my palm. Soft-blown hair drifted over his skull, so vulnerable in its fragility. My hand in the pool opened and curled upwards. After an hour he sat up and said, 'I'd better be going.' But he did not move, only peered upwards at the sky. 'She'll be wondering where I am. It's not easy to fool someone you've lived with for so long. It's difficult for me to face her sometimes.'

I had to ask him questions. It was too good a chance to miss. Harriet would be delighted when I told her.

'What do you mean, fool her?'

'Oh, you know . . . don't disappoint me, child. Fancy me going home and telling the wife I had been in the woods with you.' I said nothing and he continued, 'Will you tell your father you've been talking to me? No, of course not.'

I said for him, 'It doesn't do to tell them too much.'

'Quite.'

He began to shake the sand from his clothes, swishing his trilby hat about in the air to dry it.

'They always know there's something up,' I said. 'They know there's something, but if you don't tell them they can't be sure. But they do know. What will you tell her?'

'Oh, I don't know. She has such a dull life somehow. She belittles my coming down here to the shore, says I'm too old for that sort of thing any more. She doesn't know what sort of thing she means. Neither do I. I do no harm. I just walk down here and back again.'

'That's all Harriet and I do,' I said, not quite truthfully.

He was straightening the strands of his hair now, passing his hand restlessly over his skull. 'She'll be sitting in the dark listening to the wireless when I get in. I'll just pause in the hall, just for a moment to get my face right, even though she's in the dark. When I open the door she'll say, "It's a wonderful invention this you know, me sitting here with Max Jaffa playing just for me . . ." and I'll see how empty the room is except for her sitting on the sofa in her cardigan and sandals and the room in darkness but for the orange dial on the wireless. And you see,' he looked at me now, 'she'll know I've been talking to someone. I won't be able to hide it. It will put her out.'

'Quite,' I said, thinking how feeble he was worrying about what she thought and what she might think. It was all right me and Harriet having such qualms about our parents, we did have to pretend to conform, but at his age it was awfully flabby. I wished I could convince him of his weakness but he was already standing up, holding his hat in both hands ready to go, if not eager then anxious to get back to her. I knew he had to walk home on his own, I knew that. My father might come to meet me; she might be at her gate; but it was soft of him not daring to. I said good night and we shook hands and he began to climb the hill slope to the pines. He stumbled, nearly fell, as I watched him. I wondered if he were old. He had never looked any different even when we were children. Was he old? I lay flat in case he turned to wave to me, covering my face with my hands. I shut my eyes tight and tried to see his face in the darkness. But I could not see him clearly. I saw his head and his trilby hat, but the face was blank and smooth as glass.

3

I DID not go down to the shore again for several days. Instead I stayed at home and tried to be nice to my sister Frances. She was younger than I and quarrelsome because I had betrayed her. I had loved her dreadfully when she was very little but when she grew older and I went away to school I found my love faded. It was still there but the delight in her had gone. She had red hair and pale blue eyes and two front teeth were missing. If I teased her she cried annihilatingly; if I was gentle with her she drew back, tears of uneasy happiness in her eyes. I had to push her from me for her own sake, because of Harriet and me. I did not want her to be like us. God willing she would grow up normally and be like everyone else. But I read her some stories and praised her little crayon drawings; I helped her make clothes for her doll out of scraps of material.

Every Friday Father stayed off work to help clean out the house. He wore his old A.R.P. uniform complete with black beret and got down on his knees to scrub out the kitchen. Harriet said he was manic and that he looked like a cross between Old Mother Riley and General Montgomery. He was very dedicated; Frances and I were moved from room to room as he dusted and scoured and polished. My mother walked to the village to do a load of shopping and when Father had finished the house-work he drove off in the car to fetch her. They came back laden with cabbages and carrots, apples and toilet rolls, fresh eggs from the farm, she looking pale and exhausted, he grumbling and swearing and carrying on shouting he did too much and it wasn't right for a man to do what she expected of him. Which she didn't. She said she wished to hell he'd go out, and he said he would get out of this hell-hole once and for all one of these days. But after lunch he got the car out meekly enough and drove us to Southport for tea and cakes at Thoms'.

On the way back I shut my eyes and pretended I was out for a spin with Charles Boyer. He talked to me in his broken French and told me how lovely I was. 'O my darling you and I must nevair be parted.' We drove through Birkdale along the coast road to Hillside. When I saw the long stretch of beach I begged them to stop and let me walk home.

'Please,' I pleaded. 'You don't know how I feel at school shut away from the sea.'

They were worried for me but they could never argue with conviction. 'Don't be long,' they cried. 'Walk straight home, don't talk to strangers, don't get your feet wet,' and I was out of the car with Frances still whining to be allowed to come with me, and scrambling down the bank on to the shore.

I had to take my shoes off but I left on my stockings. My legs were so large and white. I liked it best when the wind blew strongly. I whistled and ran with my arms spread out like a bird. All the time I kept looking for interesting objects left stranded by the tide. There were no end of things Harriet and I had found. Whole crates of rotten fruit, melons and oranges and grapefruit, swollen up and bursting with salt water, lumps of meat wrapped in stained cotton sheets through which the maggots tunnelled if the weather was warm, and stranded jelly fish, purple things, obscene and mindless. Harriet drove sticks of wood into them but they were dead. Several times we found bad things, half a horse and two small dogs. They were full of water, garlanded with seaweed, snouts encrusted in salt, and teeth exposed. Their necks were tied with wire. 'They buy them for their children,' Harriet told me, 'and when they muddy up the house they bring them down here and drown them.'

At Ainsdale the shore narrowed and I went inland to the golf-course. There were more pines to walk through, growing in ragged grass beside the smooth green turf of the course. Nearby was a college for Catholic priests and I hoped one day I might meet someone from there and have a chat about religion. Harriet met a priest once but she said he was awful, his fingers stained up to the knuckles with nicotine and obviously he hadn't got a vocation because the body was a framework to the soul and his frame was dreadful.

But I met nobody.

At Freshfield, the small estuary was fouled up with mud and refuse. There were cans and bottles and paper smeared with excrement, petrol tins and ammunition containers. 'One day,' Harriet warned, 'we shall find a unborn baby still in a bag of skin on its side in the mud.' The thought both thrilled and horrified us.

Without her I did not look too closely; I did not know what I should do if the presentiment became actuality. There were two shabby boats stuck fast, never used. Nobody had the money any more.

Once on the Freshfield side of the estuary the beach ran straight to Formby and I jogged along with my shoes in my hand, thinking all the time about Harriet, about the Tsar, and a little about Charles Boyer. The tide was a long way out, the sea lay motionless; at the rim of the sky an oil tanker stayed still.

When I cut away from the seashore over the dunes to the woods, I was praying, 'Please God, oh please God,' ducking under the barbed wire and on to the cinder path, praying to God as I turned a bend in the road. I was not religious but I had a crucifix in my room and I often called on God when I was at school or away from Harriet. I just wanted something to happen.

At the gate of the Canon's house stood a group of men, standing in a circle with legs like misshapen tulips, trousers tied at the knee with string. Jimmy Demon, the Canon's gardener, was leaning against the fence and laughing.

'It's old Perjer,' he explained. 'Had a drop too much by the look of him.'

Perjer was the village recluse who lived in the sandhills with his dog, in a home made of odd planks and boxes. Harriet said he was a pederast, but I didn't really believe she knew, so I bent over him confidently and helpfully, saying to Jimmy Demon, 'I'm sure he's ill, Jimmy, he's a funny colour.'

'Dirt,' he said callously, touching the body in the dust with the toe of his boot. The men sniggered and looked sideways at me, and laughed again.

Perjer's dog sat apart, nose sniffing the air, waiting till his master should move. He turned his head suddenly with ears well forward and the Canon came out from the garden at the back of the vicarage with the Tsar. We had called the Canon senile years ago; now he seemed less so, but dribbling from the mouth and lisping as he spoke.

'Dear me, Jimmy, what is it, a meeting?'

The Tsar, with hat in hand, came nearer and looked at Jimmy.

'Drunk,' he said.

'I think he looks ill.' I turned to the Tsar. 'He almost looks as if he might be dying.'

'Rubbish.'

The dog settled down in the dust and went to sleep.

'I really think I'd better phone for the Constable to remove him . . . he can't stay here.' The canon was already purposefully moving up the path to the house. His legs were very bowed. Harriet always said to my father to annoy him 'O the canon, decent fella, been on a horse all his life'. But my father never knew what she meant.

The Tsar stood irresolute in the road. He looked at the circle of onlookers and back to the Canon fast disappearing out of sight. He passed his hand wearily over his head and said finally, 'Move him into the woods, Jimmy. He'll sleep it off. They'll only fine him at the station.'

'Reckon the Canon won't like it,' said Jimmy Demon.

Eager to show I didn't care about that, I bent too swiftly to tug at Perjer's feet. The dog swivelled in the dust and nearly caught my wrist in his teeth.

'Aaaah,' I wailed, genuinely shocked.

'O God,' the Tsar said, with disgust in his voice. 'Come on lads, get him into the trees.'

The men looked knowingly at the Tsar, picked Perjer up from the road, a welter of trousers and flapping jacket, and bundled him over the wire netting into the trees. The Tsar and I stood in the road and watched the men climb the fence and drag Perjer deeper among the pines till he was hidden. They returned and the Tsar said, 'Good, lads. We'd better be moving. Canon might not like it.'

I thought while the men were about I had better be seen going away alone, though I wanted to stay with the Tsar.

But he seemed unable to make a move. He stood, turned away from me, watching Perjer's dog run agitatedly among the trees.

Without looking at me he said, 'Let's have a look at the old fraud to see if he's comfortable.'

When I ducked quickly under the netting and waited for him I thought again he must be old. He laboured over the fence, his feet betrayed him as he alighted on the sand; he gave a little delicate sideways skip to regain his balance.

Perjer lay in a trench, one of the many left by the soldiers during the war, his head in the sand, his large hands moving frettishly over his mouth. I knelt at the side of the pit, turning my face upwards slightly so that the Tsar would see my kind expression.

'Are you feeling all right, Mr Perjer?'

There was no reply; the man's dirty face lay against the sand, the pale mouth slack.

The Tsar looked down at me. 'The police are coming,' he warned.

There were voices now in the road; we could hear the

Canon lisping out the story and the high voice of a woman, recognisable as that of the Canon's sister. We crouched down in the trench, Perjer's dog lying across the Tsar's legs.

'The Canon's sister has got wind of us.' The Tsar peeped cautiously out. Elsie stood, one capable hand on the wire netting, peering into the woods.

'O fat white woman whom nobody loves,' whispered the Tsar, and giggled nervously as he knelt in the sand.

Perjer moved his head restlessly and opened his eyes.

'He wants something,' I said, turning round awkwardly and putting my head close to the recluse.

'What is it, Mr Perjer? . . . What do you want?'

There were no voices from the road now, and the Tsar swung himself up to sit on the side of the trench, legs dangling over the edge.

'I got to piss,' said Mr Perjer very firmly, and the peevish hands struggled with his fly.

I wanted to laugh. I thought how Harriet would have stood on one leg and screamed, 'Aye, Yah! I gloat, hear me gloat!' but I pretended to be shocked, scrambling out of the trench and turning my back on the crude Mr Perjer.

The Tsar said, 'Well, there's nothing much wrong with him,' and placed his hand under my elbow and steered me away through the trees.

Sometimes late in summer Harriet and I carried what we called divining twigs, to hold before us and brush aside the webs of spiders, slung invisible from bark to bark. Now it was the Tsar who waved his hand, bestowing blessings, keeping a way clear for us. The contact of his hand on my arm was so delightful that I walked very fast, talking inarticulately and not noticing the path we travelled, till we were in the Rhododendron Lands. The Lands were private gardens and alone I should have kept to the grass verge, ready for the gardener or the squire himself, not walking in the centre of the path as I did now, alone with the Tsar. Great flowering bushes three times my height rustled on either side of us and hid the sky.

'I remember,' I began, and paused to prod the purple flowers that bounced the air and showered petals at our feet. The Tsar stood still, waving an eloquent hand to encompass the garden and the sky, and brought the movement back to his heart again.

'Never remember,' he bade me. 'It's too boring. Think of the future and the places you'll visit. Athens, child, think of Athens. I'm going to Bordeaux in the winter to bring back a barrel of wine to sweeten the dark days.'

I thought of Athens and watched his face; the lines at the corner of his mouth, the dryness of his skin as if the moisture had run out with his youth, the droop to his eyelids as if he were tired. I tried to look right inside him but nothing stayed fixed. I could only see clearly the shape of his skull and the hand placed on his heart. I sat down on the grass. I had walked a long way.

'I'll be leaving school soon.'

'What will you do then?'

'I might go to art school . . . if my Dad lets me.'

I knew I wouldn't. It was Harriet who drew well, not me. It was Harriet who was educated; she told me what to read, explained to me the things I read, told me what painters I should admire and why. I listened, I did as she said, but I did not feel much interest, at least not on my own, only when she was directing me.

'Why not come to Bordeaux with me?'

I wanted to shout with laughter. I sang wildly to myself, 'Here we go again Sister Jane.' It was just it was so marvellous to be asked by a nearly old man, thirty inches round the belly-o, to go to Bordeaux to collect a barrel of wine for the winter.

Aloud I said, 'Oh, I couldn't, I haven't any money. Thank you very much for asking though.'

Then we could not talk any more because I had been out hours and they would be worried at home and perhaps having a row over me, spoiling their supper with words. All the way home I kept repeating to myself, 'O I couldn't, God, surely I couldn't'.

But I felt I could.

4

O N Sunday morning I went to church. My mother nearly spoilt it by making me wear a hat, but I took it off in the road and carried it. I knew very well what I should look like if I wore it, because Harriet had told me on previous occasions: like an old maid at a flower show. I met the retired postman in the lane who tried to delay me. He balanced dubiously on his bicycle, feet splayed out to steady himself. 'Hallo, hallo, hallo.' He was able to go on like this for ever, like a small child knowing simple words. 'Hallo, hallo, fancy seeing you! What a bonny girl you're growing . . . fancy . . .'

I said, 'Hallo, hallo', and thought it daring, but then Harriet was not with me.

'I've had an upset,' the postman said confidingly. 'Mother, you know. Yes, I heard a bump, thought she'd dropped something, she's always dropping things, but when I went to look I couldn't open the door. She was flat out. I had to push the door, I can tell you. She's a big woman, and there she was with a great crack in her head.'

'How awful.'

A woman passed on a small bicycle, engulfing it ponderously. 'Hallo, hallo,' cried the postman, but there was no reply. 'Mrs Biggs,' he said, turning round on his seat and nearly toppling over.

It wasn't till after lunch when my mother asked me if I had seen anyone I knew in church that I remembered Mrs Biggs. The woman on the bike that the postman had called out to, was the wife of the Tsar. I went to my room and lay down on the bed, trying to think what she looked like. Big, taller than he was and grey haired; that meant she was old. And a tweed coat with a belt on. Big legs. That was all. Mrs Biggs was the one who had told my mother about me and Harriet being on the shore with Italian prisoners.

'Mother!' I opened the door and stood on the landing. I could hear her saying something to Frances in the room below.

'Mother!'

The kitchen door opened. The door knob rattled as my mother leant her weight on it. I imagined her bland face peering inquiringly into the hall.

'Yes, dear.'

'Was it Mrs Biggs from Timothy Street who said we were meeting Italian prisoners?'

I felt very brave mentioning it. Of course Harriet had lied so convincingly that my father had said Mrs Biggs was a dangerous woman, but Mother had seemed very cool with me for weeks afterwards.

'Yes, I think so. Why?' At once my mother was curious. If I wasn't quick she would be upstairs to have a little chat with me. 'Oh nothing. I thought I saw her this morning, that's all.'

I waited a moment then went back to my bedroom and shut the door. So that was her. She had seen Harriet a year ago in the arms of an Italian prisoner. I was behind a sandhill with another one and she only heard my voice. She told my mother that Harriet was a bad influence but she never went to Harriet's parents. Harriet had met her in the street and told her to mind her own business. She was so angry that the woman recoiled from her. But if Mrs Biggs spotted me with the Tsar she would come round right away and there would be no Harriet to defend me.

I felt despair. I could not bear it when my mother was angry. When I had been little it had been different. Small sins expiated by flurried scoldings and smacked bottoms. I was not frightened of her anger, just distressed by the futility of her emotions.

I waited anxiously till tea was over and walked to the

church knowing I would meet the Tsar. It was raining again and we sat in the church porch, our feet resting on the tomb of a Norman soldier, arguing listlessly about the importance of things. I said that the historic body beneath us was a thing of reverence. After all, he had gone on about the ruins of Greece but all he said was, 'Nonsense, just a heap of bones.'

'It's romantic.'

He looked gloomily out at the green-drenched world and said, 'Do you think so, do you really think so?'

When I had nearly found the words to tell him about Mrs Biggs and that it would be better if we did not meet again, he said, 'I was married here. Held the wedding breakfast where you're sitting.' How harsh, I thought, listening in the porch to an old man's recollections.

'I put on my dark suit,' began the Tsar, blowing cigarette smoke before his face, 'and she had a coffee-coloured dress, very short, and pointed shoes with straps. We walked here from Timothy Street and her mother and the Canon sat in the back of the church while we were married. A friend of mine, Arthur, performed the ceremony, gliding and cavorting up the altar steps. Those days,' he said, looking out at the poplars blowing wetly by the Canon's fence, 'they hadn't got graves all round the church. Instead there were trees, great tall elms that shut out the light. There were protests about cutting them down but the arguments were sound enough. Had to cut them down, there were too many dead to bury. I could hardly see Arthur but for the white smock he wore; he looked like a moth in the darkness. Then we came outside and her mother unwrapped the cake she had made, and she and the Canon and the wife ate most of it sitting where you are now. I didn't have any. I wasn't hungry.'

He fell silent. I could not move. I stared at the ground expecting to see crumbs dropped effortlessly from the Canon's mouth, but there was nothing.

I felt sleepy; a great heaviness filled me. He was old.

All those years we had known him and never once was he young. We had smiled fleetingly, nodded our heads; he had raised his trilby hat and waved to us as we wandered down the lane towards the sea and all the time we grew and he stayed motionless. Twenty years before we were born, at random almost, he had married Mrs Biggs.

The Tsar said, 'She was pretty, you know,' and I waited. His voice had grown small, he was talking out loud to himself.

'No, not pretty. Big, full, her throat was . . . her hair smelled . . . those lovely kisses . . .'

I coughed, it was too embarrassing listening to him. He turned and said, 'We did our courting here you know. We met under the lamp under the tree.'

'Indeed.' Primly I swung my legs above the tomb and hunched my shoulders.

'Lots of evenings in the rain . . . the struggling under the beech leaves . . . the talking we did . . . the promises we made . . . you do, you know, and you mean it . . . the smell of the grass . . . I thought . . .'

I had to lean forward to hear him. I did not want to hear but I had to.

'I thought her legs were made of pearl, dappled under the trees . . . when we heard a rustle in the grass I would know it was a bird or an animal, not a man prying and I would lean back tenderly, saying, "*Keine mensch*, my love, *keine mensch*" . . . and now our dancing days are over.'

He cleared his throat, looked at me speculatively and turned away. I wished with all my might that he had never been. My eyes seemed so wide open in the rain; I felt I would never be happy again. The woman cycling down the road, all her promises turned to fat, the vast legs obscenely dappled under the beech leaves thirty years ago, the marionette doll on the bench, head dangling, eyes filled with sentimental tears, they walked the graveyard together.

The thought came to me that if I touched his mouth with mine it would taste salt from all the years he had walked up and down, up and down the lane to the sea.

'I will walk away now,' I told myself fiercely. 'I will walk away now.'

The Tsar said musingly, 'It must be getting late. We'd better go our separate ways.'

I said good night. I said it so normally I surprised myself. We parted at the cross-roads near the Canon's house; the Tsar to go down the avenue of pines towards the railway crossing, and I across the fields to the station. I waited under the lamp until he turned and waved his trilby hat in farewell, a dark figure whose dancing days were over. Then I began to run home, shouting out loudly in the empty field, 'God bless me, Harriet . . . come home.'

5

HARRIET came home two days later. She whistled outside our house and sat on the wall farther down the road. I was so pleased to see her I did not notice how withdrawn she was. I looked at her clever face with joy and told her about the Tsar, and she listened kicking the wall with thin legs and rubbing her arms all the time.

They were sunburned and the skin was peeling. I waited for her shout of surprise, expecting her to jump off the wall and hop about the lane, but she just sat there rubbing her arms.

'He said' – surely she would look at me now – 'he said that he and I should go to Bordeaux to fetch a barrel of wine for the winter.'

Harriet said 'Oh' politely and looked down at her body complacently. I was silent.

A man was mowing the lawn opposite; he walked neatly up and down. The blossom on the mock-almond trees behind the wall drooped a little and fluttered in the breeze. A petal fell curled tight on Harriet's neck, and she shook herself quickly.

'I met a boy in Wales,' she said. 'He's nineteen.'

I was embarrassed; yet I wanted to ask her questions. It was only fair; I had told her everything about the Tsar, though of course that was funny. It was meant to be comic, so I laughed.

Harriet got down from the wall very carefully, and began to walk up the lane to her house.

29

'Please, Harriet.' I tried to catch hold of her arm. 'Please, Harriet, what's wrong?'

'I just want to be quiet . . . It's so hot.'

I stopped helpless, watching her walk away, and climbed back on the wall again. If she looked round she would see how hurt I was, so I hung my head dejectedly, but when I finally looked up she had gone. After tea I went upstairs and washed my face, and dabbed some of Mother's powder on my cheeks; but it made my face look grey almost, so I rubbed it off on the towel.

I looked so different from the frail way I felt. A noble nose and a pale bold mouth, robust limbs and crinkly hair. My mother had it permanently waved every year, and because I ran about energetically it hung messily over my forehead making me look sullen. It also smelled when it rained. I thought I looked lumpy and middle-aged, but I smiled resourcefully and said, 'God bless me and make me beautiful,' and combed my hair with care.

Harriet was in her bedroom; she saw me from the window and came down to open the front door.

'Hallo, you.' She smiled. The small irregular teeth showed. She was all pleasantness.

'Come on up.' She led the way upstairs to the small dark bedroom. We sat on the floor, Harriet leaning against the bed and rubbing her sunburned arms.

'What's all this about the Tsar?' she asked.

I told her the story all over again, but left out the bit about the wine. It was too good a thing to risk telling Harriet in her present state.

Now Harriet understood the importance of my news; she lay on the floor encouragingly, kicking her legs in the air. I was so triumphant I forgot her earlier mood and described the sallow neck beneath the collar.

Harriet's voice rose higher. 'It's probably dead white after that bit. Like something under a stone. You see it in the summer always when men open their shirts, and they're grey underneath.'

We both shuddered and Harriet raised her arms victoriously. 'That's the colour to be, burnt all over,' and she sat up and rubbed them. I wished she had not said that. She knew I was never anything but white. Even when the sun was so hot, Harriet was a deep brown, I stayed white.

Harriet knelt upright, drew out a box from under the dresser, opened it and handed me the diary. 'We've neglected it,' she said as I took it. 'I've lots to write about.'

While she found a pencil I looked at the last entry. 'We have both read D. H. Lawrence's *Lost Girl*,' I had written. 'We find it very fine and imagine Italians make good lovers.'

Harriet gave me the pencil and lay on the floor again.

'Put, "She has been away in Wales".'

I began to write and kept my face averted, trying to be neat and quick at the same time.

'She has been away in Wales. What next?'

'Put, "I have been here alone".' Harriet's voice was muffled against the carpet. 'And that you have become more intimate with the Tsar.' It was always Harriet who dictated the diary, but it was in my writing in case her mother discovered it. 'She might read something of mine,' Harriet had explained, 'but not if it was strange handwriting.' We never mentioned names and everyone had a pseudonym, to be the more safe.

'She,' Harriet said, 'has made an illuminating discovery. She has met a boy of nineteen . . . no.' Harriet sat up. 'Put "a man" instead, don't put the age. "He has yellow hair and is devoid of humour, but she found him very interesting".'

She stood up and combed her hair at the dressing table, peering at her face and leaning her elbows on the dresser top to get a closer view.

'Look,' she bade me. 'Look at my bottom lip, it's bruised.'

Before I could look she turned hurriedly away and began to dictate with her back to me.

'Her lip is bruised. It is a queer brown colour and swollen from underneath where he kissed her. He made her face rough too.'

I wrote it all down and felt dismayed at the sentences. Not

31

that the diary contained no other such passages, but Harriet was taking pleasure in dictating and telling me simultaneously. Always before we had both discussed things to go in the diary, analysed emotions, looked in the dictionary for suitable words, and fashioned the paragraphs sentence by sentence.

'We've got to be scientific,' Harriet had said. 'Otherwise we'll find it merely smutty on reading.'

'Go on,' I said, anxious to hear more.

'We lay down in a field near a farmhouse one day . . .'

I could not look up, I held the pencil so tight my fingers ached.

'Yes,' I said.

'He kissed me and hurt my mouth, then he put his hand on my neck and . . .' She broke off quickly and turned. 'Oh, give it to me, I'll write it.'

I could only sit there watching her scribble across the page, a deep frown of concentration on her face, her bottom lip slightly swollen. When she had finished she shut the book, placed it in the box and thrust it under the dresser. Seeing my face she said kindly, 'You can read it next time. Don't worry, it's nothing really. Let's go down to the sea.'

'Yes,' I said miserably, and waited for her to apply lipstick.

Harriet was a year older than I but looked much younger, with plaits fastened round her head. I was thirteen but I looked ancient beside Harriet, with my permed hair and plump body. Harriet never wore hats except sometimes an old straw panama when it rained. My spirits returned as we walked down the lane. I clutched at Harriet and laughed nervously. 'Don't laugh, he'll be there, he always is, just you see. Oh, don't laugh.'

Harriet haughtily turned her face to the sky and said in her special society voice, 'I'm sure I don't know what you mean, dear.'

And while we laughed and swayed down the lane we caught sight of the Tsar leaning against the lamp by the Canon's fence, head craned forward on the thin discoloured neck, hat in hand.

'Now, now,' said Harriet busily approaching him. 'What's all this. Can't have followers, you know.'

'Oh Harriet, really,' I said watching the Tsar's amused contemptuous face.

Harriet and the Tsar walked together, and I followed a little way behind them through the trees. Now and then I heard the Tsar say, 'And you think so?', and saw Harriet shake her head vehemently. I hoped they were talking about me but suddenly Harriet broke away from the path and jumped to swing on a branch, and shouted, red in the face, 'He's nineteen.'

I stopped and looked up at her in disbelief. Her feet clear of the ground threatened to kick me over.

'Move,' she ordered. 'Go on, move.'

She pushed at my chest with both feet and I stumbled and fell backward. Harriet let go of the branch and stood over me, her dress rumpled, one plait beginning to slide from its position, her face defiant.

'I told you to move, I did warn you.' She held out her hand but I just lay there refusing to look at her.

'Well, all right, sulk.' She stood undecided. 'When you feel more sensible I'll be near the tadpole pools.'

I sat up then and watched her go, brushing pine-needles from my frock dejectedly.

'She's a hot-tempered girl.' The Tsar squatted on his haunches a little distance from me, and swung his hat between his knees.

I wanted to tell him he didn't know what he was talking about; that he ought to have learnt more about people than to say she was hot-tempered.

Instead I stood up and rubbed the side of my leg patterned with pine-needles, and looked down at him balanced on his heels like a dancer. Perhaps not so old after all, even if he wasn't nineteen like the boy in Wales.

'Come on, Tsar,' I said. 'Let's find Harriet.'

But he only rocked a little where he crouched and looked at me with light eyes.

33

'I want to tell you something.'

'What? I want to find Harriet.'

The Tsar stood up and came close to me, and I turned in the direction Harriet had gone and saw the sun had drawn level with the trees and circled them with flames.

Please God (I could feel the Tsar's hand on my shoulder) please God send Harriet. Then I turned to face the tiger. So dingy he was with his sallow skin and thin hair brushed carefully back. For all his elegance, and graceful walk, the delicate way he moved his head, indefinably he lacked youth. Later I was to remember the stillness in the woods, the evening in an avenue of light between the tree trunks, and the Tsar with his hand on my shoulder. I did not know I loved him then, because as Harriet wrote later in the diary, we had a long way to go before we reached the point of love.

The Tsar moved himself worriedly and took my fingers between his own. 'No, no,' he said under the pines, as if he had read my thoughts, 'No, child, no,' and with a sudden clumsy movement pulled my head against his shoulder. I stood there awkwardly straddled, not daring to ease myself away, but turning my face gently to gaze alone the avenue of light. He stood back so suddenly I almost stumbled, and he walked away shouting in his high amused voice, 'Harriet, where art thou?'

Harriet told me afterwards she had seen it all, and that I looked most uncomfortable, but when we reached the edge of the trees she was sitting a long way down the slope with her back to us. Her plaits hung about her ears, she sat without shoes, the bony feet curled under the sand. She looked cold all over.

I sat down beside her and nudged her arm but she would not look at me. The Tsar stood above us; we could hear him breathing heavily from the effort of the climb. I wanted to shout, to laugh, to roll in the sand; anything to throw off the awful weighty responsibility I felt. Always before the feeling had been occasioned by Harriet, by something she had made me do. The time she had borrowed the hand-cart from Mr

34

Redman and wheeled me up and down the lane crying, 'Bring out your dead,' I had lain crushed and embarrassed with pain. I had smiled and shown my splendid teeth, clutching tight to the side of the barrow and wishing to die. But that had come to an end when we put the cart back in the garage. The Tsar would not be so easily disposed of; and the putting away in the end would be up to me, not Harriet.

When we wrote in the diary later that night, Harriet told me to use a new page so that I should not see what she had written earlier about the boy in the field. What she had dictated about the Tsar seemed to both of us inarticulate. But it was so difficult.

I wrote . . .

The Tsar tried to kiss me, I think; but nothing happened. She hid behind the sandhills and thought I looked very uncomfortable. I should have stood closer, then I would not have felt so foolish.

Then Harriet told me to write the bit about love, and how we had not tasted everything yet. Before she shut me out in the garden I held the door open, whispering in case her mother overheard.

'What haven't we tasted yet?'

'Oh many things. You wait.'

Then her mother joined us on the step, talking pleasantly and emptily. Harriet put an arm round her waist and looked fondly at her, but it was unconvincing. We both tried very hard to give our parents love, and security, but they were too demanding.

I said good night, and walked home down the lane pointing my feet at every step, craning my neck the better to see the stars.

6

'I ASK you dear,' said Harriet rolling over on to her stomach, holding her plait up to the sunlight. 'Is it likely that a woman would admit to being jealous of a girl of thirteen?'

'I suppose not.' I sounded unconvinced. 'But supposing she did admit it and came round to our house to see Mother. Think of the row there'd be.'

Harriet lay still and serious. 'You could always say Mrs Biggs was perverted. After all, it's a nasty thing to imply.'

'But Mother,' I insisted. 'She's hardly forgotten the Italians yet.'

'Good Lord,' Harriet sat up amazed. 'That was years ago. We may have been precocious but it was innocent enough.' She looked round the field. 'Wasn't it?'

I tried to think what innocence meant and failed.

'I don't know if we were ever innocent.' I hoped I sounded casual in case we became embarrassed and pedantic.

'Well, we felt daring the time we met the prisoners.' Harriet was annoyed. 'We were awfully scared. That's innocence. Why, you said you didn't want to go the second time, and I went alone and said you were ill. What happened to you?'

I stared at the poppies by the fence, the stiff hairy stems that wavered when the flower burst. In bud they stood fierce and firm; once wanton in the sun they flowered and grew weak. I nearly told Harriet I felt like that but it seemed too vague and sentimental. 'I just went for a walk along the shore.' I lay back in the grass.

'You should have come,' said Harriet. 'It was interesting.'

I had read the diary so I knew it was interesting. Instead I had walked along the edge of the sea, picking up shells and rolling burst melons soggily over the sand.

The first time we had met the prisoners I had been uneasy but not frightened. Harriet had asked them questions about their families and country, and they had shown us photographs. Sedate images of brothers and mothers, and one of a girl with a cross on a chain around her neck. 'Anna-Maria,' the younger one pointed at the photograph. 'Very beautiful girl . . . like you.' And he smiled at Harriet. The older man was plump and short with a neat nose and tiny ears that lay flat against his head. The last time we had gone to meet them, the time Mrs Biggs saw us, Harriet told me to take the plump man away somewhere on my own.

Walking in the sun along the sand, shirt torn open, arms spread high, feet wet and cold in the sea. Sliding damp skinned over green moss, alive and moving on the rocks by the concrete hangers. Walking behind the sandhills and sitting with bare feet beside the plump Italian. He called me 'a dirty little angel'. Adolescent tremblings, swirls of nerves gone gold. The pain of the moment, the awful uncontrolled joy; that was innocence.

I sat up in the field and said loudly, 'Remember, Harriet, he called me a dirty little angel.'

'Mmmm.' Harriet face downwards in the grass was in a private dream of her own.

We were in the field behind my house, screened from the garden where Mother sat reading a library book, by a row of tattered poplars that stood close to the fence. As the wind lifted them lightly I could see my mother's deck-chair, and the problem of Mrs Biggs came uneasily to my mind.

'Harriet. Harriet . . . Listen.'

'What?'

'We shall have to be very careful,' I said, lying down beside her. She turned and her breath came sweetly against my face.

37

'We shall have to drop a hint now and then of seeing the Tsar on our walks, so that if Mrs Biggs does arrive our lies will seem more plausible.'

'Very well,' said Harriet. 'But discreetly, just in general conversation. "Oh, I saw Mr Biggs last night, he does look ill," or something like that.'

'And you tell him not to speak to us in the lane.' I warned her.

'It does seem a little unnecessary.' Harriet lay on her back and covered her face with her arm. 'You've got nothing out of it so far.' I felt angry with her. He had told me all his fragile history; told me of his wedding day, and his summer evenings. He had said by the tadpole pools . . . She'll know I've been happy tonight . . . I could not forget that he trusted me. Aloud I said:

'It might be best to finish the whole adventure, just not follow it up.'

But I knew I could not do that, even if Harriet allowed me. A year ago, to be called a Dirty Little Angel would have kept us going for months. Now it was not enough; more elaborate things had to be said; each new experience had to leave a more complicated tracery of sensations; to satisfy us every memory must be more desperate than the last.

In the beginning we had never searched for experience. True we didn't follow the usual childish pursuits. We never played games or behaved like playmates, we never verbally abused each other except on occasions deliberately, to reassure our parents. It was Dodie who began it, telling us of the gay times she had known in her youth, without Papa guessing. 'Making the friendly gesture' she had called it. And we liked her stories, we were fascinated. We took to going for long walks over the shore, looking for people who by their chosen solitariness must have something to hide. We learnt early it was the gently resigned ones who had the most to tell; the voluble and frantic were no use. They seldom got beyond pity for themselves and at the end mouthed soft obscenities. At first Harriet was interrogator and I spectator. When she questioned adults and probed their lives I was content to listen. She said we were not to become involved, we were too young, only to learn. She said our information was a kind of training course for later life; living at second hand was our objective until we were old enough. But of late, even at school and away from Harriet's influence, the process of analysis went on. It had become a habit: the steady search to discover the background of teachers; the singling out of girls older than myself who might add something to what I already knew.

Progressively it became less of a joy when the girl would say, as one had, 'It's so hard to be good now, isn't it? Mummy says it will be much easier when I'm grown up.' I thought of the sins of my childhood; the hats lost on train journeys, the gloves left behind in church, the refusal to go on a message. I thought of the things I had done since, things that Harriet and I did not consider strange, but that would rank as enormities to this girl . . . and my mother. Harriet told me that in other lands, in other cultures, in other times, both past and in the future, we would not be thought abnormal, but it did not help. I was separated from my mother by an invisible wall, a wall of amyl, that had become no longer hypothetical. Never again to share little jokes with her, to sit in the garden peacefully waiting for the apples to ripen and summer to bloom.

Harriet stood up in the field and stretched her body, arms above her head.

'Your mother's calling . . . tea I think.'

'Coming, Mother,' I shouted.

We climbed the fence and walked down the garden towards my smiling mother. She told me to fetch deck-chairs from the green-house. Through the glass I spied on them both, Harriet at my mother's feet, looking up winningly into her face. The smell in the green-house assumed shape and colour; the stuffy green of the tomato plants, the bursting splitting red of the fruit, the pale grey odour of last year's mint hanging from a nail above the door. I was too warm, too indolent to bother any more about Mrs Biggs. If she came and told my mother stories and Mother suffered, it was not I that was to blame.

But when I looked through the glass and saw her sitting there so happy on her scarlet deck-chair, she was my best beloved and I wished she need not suffer.

'Hurry up!' she called.

She asked me to sit on the deck-chair but I wouldn't. I sat on the grass and drank my tea. Harriet did as she was asked and chatted eagerly for my benefit. To cover my silence.

'Yes, I'm specialising in maths now.' She looked fully into my mother's eyes. 'Of course, it's only a means to an end, I'm more interested in science you know.'

A wasp hovered erratically above the lupins, turned suspended in the air, and spun buzzing to the fallen apples beneath the flower.

Harriet was saying, 'We saw Mr Biggs last night. He looked ill, we thought. Didn't we?'

'Oh, I don't know, perhaps a little pale . . . but I hardly know him.'

'I thought you used to be great pals.' My mother refilled my cup, her eyes kind and loving. 'You got a card from him once.'

'Did I?' I looked at Harriet but she avoided my gaze.

Sometimes in a mood of contentment and affection I confided things to my mother. Usually I had reason to regret it.

Harriet was carefully putting her tea-leaves in the grass. She looked up and said slowly, 'You never told me . . . you must have quite a collection by now.'

'A collection of what?'

'Cards, dear,' she said.

'From Mr Biggs?' My mother was puzzled.

'Oh, don't be daft, Harriet.' Crossly I pinched her leg and scowled at her.

'I always remember,' Harriet continued, 'the ones you received from Rome and Naples and all points north.'

My mother was looking at her and then at me.

'I do think you should shut up, I do think you might.'

'Perhaps I got it wrong,' said Harriet contritely. 'Perhaps it was someone else.'

After a little pause she went on, 'I do remember you got one once from Mrs Biggs.'

I very nearly laughed at the absurdity of the lie.

'I met her at the station the day she was posting it,' Harriet spoke severely, 'and she said – was it *Berks* or *Barks*?'

'I shouldn't have thought' – Mother was thinking of the Italians – 'that Mrs Biggs would send you a card.'

It was beyond me now. I relaxed and let Harriet extricate me as best she could, seeing my mother's face as if through a curtain of gauze. I saw her opening her small mouth primly and beautifully, but I heard no sound in the garden. A cloud began to roll softly towards the sun; the lupin beds already were cold and shut off from the light; the grass a little way down the garden faded while I watched.

The shadow crept steadily up the lawn, extinguishing the roses, the holly bush, the apple tree beside the fence. Only Mother and Harriet lingered, glowing in a corner of light; then they too wavered, struggled with invisible shutters, and turned grey. I waited. The cloud disintegrated in the sky, the grass brightened and Harriet enveloped herself in the warmth again.

The back gate loudly closed; the small figure of Frances pushed its way through the privet hedge.

'Don't,' called Mother. 'Walk round, dear.'

But Frances was already coming sideways up the lawn, trailing her coat along the ground.

'Hallo, Harriet,' she said politely, and stood leaning against my mother's knees.

I could see the next-door neighbour looking through the kitchen window into our garden. We must have made a charming group. Tea on the lawn, the mother surrounded by children, the clear voices. At least we looked real. Even if Harriet and I were alien it could not show.

'Let's take a photograph,' my mother said. 'I've a new film in the dining-room drawer.'

'I'll get it.' Frances was running down the garden.

At the privet hedge she swerved and ran along the rockery

to the concrete path. Her face appeared at the kitchen window. 'Thought I was going through the hedge, didn't you, Mummy?'

My mother smiled indulgently and Harriet and I smiled too with relief.

When we sat on the grass, Frances between us, I hoped for a moment the camera would not work.

'Look up, Frances.' My mother waited and the shutter clicked.

What if the film exposed not three children in the sun, but one between two spectres, wearing childish smiles. Faces that crumbled like bread in the fingers, and showed a fearful disintegration. Harriet wanted to take a photograph of mother and myself, but I said no, so she placed Frances between my mother's knees and looked professionally at the group.

'Put your arm round her neck,' she told Frances.

Here at least would be a record of all that was true and good and beautiful.

When the photographing was finished Frances knelt on the grass beside me, putting her arms round my neck, and rubbing her face against mine.

'There's a fair on at Bumpy field tomorrow, isn't there? There's roundabouts and a menagerie, isn't there? Please take me, please.'

My mother looked pleadingly at me and then at Harriet.

'Do take her with you, she does so want to go. It will only be for half an hour.'

'And then I shall have to leave and bring her back I suppose.'

I was angry too quickly. A fierce irritation caused me to shake Frances away from me.

The more kindly and generously my mother looked at me, the more irritated I grew.

'It's so stupid. Just because you won't take her yourself, I have to. Why can't she be more self-contained. I don't beg always to be with other people.'

'But you've Harriet.' Frances began to cry desperately, sobbing terribly on the grass, her whole body given to sudden grief.

Harriet said, 'Thank you for the tea, I must be going now. We'll take you to the fair, don't cry, Frances.'

My mother looked gratefully at her, but still she didn't reproach me.

At the gate Harriet watched me almost with distaste.

'Why do you get so illogical? It's so ugly when you allow them to disturb you.'

I must have looked very close to despair at this, for she added in her society voice, 'Rise above it, dear . . . rise above it.'

'Are we going to the shore tonight?' I asked.

Three high-bosomed women in hard bowler hats, sitting penguin-shaped on three fleshy horses, appeared at the corner of the lane. Massive and leisurely they passed our gate, filling the lane with tweed jackets and cello thighs.

Harriet looked at the group thoughtfully. 'No, I've something special to do tonight. I'll tell you tomorrow.'

She began to walk unhurriedly away from me, her sandals making no sound on the road; in the garden at the back of the house, Frances, her grief forgotten, could be heard screaming with laughter.

7

H ARRIET went directly home to her father.

He was a tall man, very morose, possessing a fierce sense of justice and great sentimentality. To hear *Roses of Picardy* or *Silver Threads Among the Gold* filled him with emotion. He would talk constantly to Harriet with immense nostalgia of his youth and his brother William. His childhood it would seem had been a hard one. 'The cruelty of those days,' he was fond of saying, 'the ignorance.' It was therefore surprising to us that any misdemeanour on Harriet's part, however slight, brought instant physical chastisement.

She liked to do helpful jobs for him. Filling the watering can when he ill-humouredly worked in the garden, finding his cigarettes for him when he mislaid them; taking a certain satisfaction in thus soothing his irritable mind.

Though he was strict about her school work, and displeased if she fell back a place in her form, he was relaxed in other respects. She could in summer stay out long after it was dark, go swimming in the salt sea off the Point, where the soldiers splashed every morning and the nuns from the convent shyly billowed out over the sheeted water of an evening, and he even allowed her to go without breakfast if she so wished.

Harriet had made tea for her father, her mother being in town that afternoon, and told him about Frances wanting me to take her to the fair. She said I had shouted at my mother and quite lost control. Her father said, nodding his head wisely, 'I used to be the same myself; it's all part of the process of wanting to do without guidance and control. I remember

44

I told my mother once, and she was a very hasty woman, that she ought not to rely on me to entertain William. "Mother," I said, "Willam must realise I'm almost a man and learn to stay with you." I was eighteen and been out working for four years, but she gave me a blow across the head with her hand that made me shout. I can feel it now. But she was right you know.'

Harriet pretended to agree with him, and waited till he had come to the end of his reminiscences. Then she said casually she had heard Mr Biggs was ill.

Her father was immediately alarmed, fearing that his Saturday round of golf was in jeopardy.

'Run round and see if it's anything serious,' he told her. 'And find out if he'll be well enough for Saturday.'

Harriet, pleased with her strategy, wheeled her mother's bicycle out of the shed, and rode to Timothy Street.

The Tsar's house was a large Victorian-fronted building, with overgrown gardens back and front. The front gate was large and solid, painted black and so tall it was impossible to see over. Though it was summer and not yet six o'clock there was a light in the front room, and one curtain was drawn a quarter of the way across the large windows; this and the row of thick holly bushes made the light necessary. It was such a neglected house, dark and well made, unlike the houses we lived in, strung like cherry-stones along the lane, that Harriet expected the door to swing open on its hinges without human help. While she was waiting curiously for this to happen, voices were raised in argument somewhere in the house. For a moment she thought her lie had become truth, that Mrs Biggs was quarrelling with the Tsar come home ill from work. Then she realised it was the wireless and lifting the knocker firmly rapped it against the door.

Mrs Biggs, in fawn cardigan and sandals, like those we wore, opened the door, heaving it backwards and staring full at Harriet.

She led her with one hand down the hall, the other to her lips. 'Silence,' she whispered. 'It's such a good play.'

Like characters before the Tabs in a pantomime, tiptoeing

45

across the stage to fill in a difficult transformation scene, they entered the front-room.

Harriet sat on the sofa, knees close together, Mrs Biggs in an armchair by the fire leaning forward, giving her whole attention to the radio. The clock on the mantelpiece said half past five, and listening for a moment to the sense of the words spoken, Harriet realised it was Children's Hour.

The room as she later described it, was heavy and cumbersome with furniture. A huge Welsh dresser against the wall, with a mirror panel partly screened by plates in blue and gold; a sideboard near the window with a statue on its top, brandishing a sword and with one feminine breast rakishly exposed. What made the statue command attention, said Harriet, was not its size which was formidable, but the statue's nipple which was tipped with scarlet. The rest of the room was dark and very warm. Gradually, as Harriet later described it, between Mrs Biggs and herself grew a hedge of green ivy. She saw through the leaves the mouth of the Tsar's wife open giddily as she sat listening to a children's entertainment. Her hands in her lap closed idly and heavily, in and out, sleep-laden like a red-rusted weed in the sea.

The face of Mrs Biggs was large and dry; light-coloured eyes set flat in her head, grey thick hair rolled up above her ears and neck.

'Have you had tea, dear?' she asked when the programme came to an end.

'Yes, thank you.'

Mrs Biggs stood up and poked the fire with a brass curtain rod; as she leant forward Harriet could see on the calves of her legs strong black hairs. She was watching Harriet through the mirror above the fireplace.

Harriet who was fond of assuming the character expected of her in certain different houses, now became the large girl at the Christmas party, arms crossed over a growing chest, her eyes wide open and greedy.

'Father sent me to ask if Mr Biggs will be calling for him as usual this Saturday. He'd heard that he wasn't well.'

46

Mrs Biggs received this last piece of news with less surprise than expected.

'Oh, he'll be able to play golf all right. There's nothing wrong with him that I know of.'

Her eyes strayed to the small table by the lamp, with its array of bottles and syphon.

'A little self-control would be a help.'

Harriet began to hate Mrs Biggs, sitting there untidily in a stained cardigan, talking of self-control.

'He's weak,' said Mrs Biggs, as if to excuse herself. 'His mother told me as much years ago, but somehow you don't pay attention to that sort of thing when you're young.'

She reached up and took a silver-framed photograph down from the mantelpiece and handed it to Harriet.

'Look at that!'

It was a young face, rather smooth and old-fashioned, with oiled hair brushed well back.

'It's Mr Biggs,' said Harriet. 'I never knew he wore spectacles.'

'He became vainer as he grew older. Strains his eyes all the time, but won't wear glasses.' Her face began to change in expression; she wanted Harriet to go now. Her eyes darkened with impatience, her hands fidgeted in her lap. But Harriet would not go. She told me, 'I knew she wanted me to go, and that made it so that I couldn't.'

Stubbornly she held the photograph and tried to see some faint trace in it of the Tsar we knew. She was aware of Mrs Biggs, restless and suddenly tired in her armchair by the fire; voices in the lane outside made the room isolated and withdrawn.

Looking up suddenly at Mrs Biggs, she was aware of an expression half formed in the woman's light eyes, something of cunning or sadness that was wholly unconscious.

'How's that little friend of yours?' Mrs Biggs asked. 'The stout one. Getting on all right at that school?'

'Yes, thank you. I think so.'

Harriet stood up, placed the young Tsar on the mantelpiece

47

and turned to go. In the hall it was cool; the door into the garden opened to show the pale washed sky; the holly bush near the porch quivered, stabbing green leaves upwards in the warm air. Mrs Biggs waited till Harriet had successfully manoeuvred her bicycle out into the road; she gave a small, not unfriendly smile, and stepped into the house. Then she shut the door.

It was the following night when, Frances between us, we walked to Bumpy field, that Harriet told me of her visit to the house of the Tsar.

We had to be very careful in case Frances repeated what she heard but, as she ran ahead every few moments in her excitement to reach the fair, we felt there was little danger of her understanding such disjointed conversation as ours.

'I wish,' I said kindly to Harriet, 'I had seen the photograph.'

I did not mean it, for though I considered Harriet brave and clever I almost hated her for prising Mrs Biggs open in that way. I imagined the woman's heart laid bare, the cancerous growth of bitterness dissected coldly; as for the photograph, why that was no more the Tsar than I was the frail golden girl I dreamed of being.

Harriet laughed suddenly. 'She called you stout, you know. "Your stout friend" she said.'

I was suddenly afraid lest Mrs Biggs should describe me so to the Tsar. He may not have noticed it before, and then aware of his wife's remark turn slowly to me one day under the church porch, saying, 'You are stout, aren't you?'

Frances ran back again to meet us, hopping on one leg and holding with both hands to my arm.

'You can hear the music,' she said.

A little way past the paper shop and between a row of cottages lay Bumpy field, circled with noise and military bands.

Above the loudspeaker music and the excited cries of Frances I heard Harriet say, 'I kept thinking of Wales when I was sitting with her. Not the boy with the yellow hair, but the country. I kept seeing it.'

48

'Perhaps he'll be here,' I said, thinking of the Tsar, as we turned along the path to the field.

A man in shirt-sleeves sat heedlessly in the rain on a three-legged stool in the grass, before a small table. He gave us tickets without looking up from the paper he was reading, making a small flapping movement with it when Harriet leaned too heavily against the table.

'Don't,' I admonished her, hoping he would look up, and I would be able to tell instantly if he thought me stout. But he paid no attention, just sat there head down, the rain moulding his black hair like a cap about his ears, and read his paper.

Small gusts of wind eddied down the field; the air was filled with sharp intakes of breath; children and girls screamed uniformly, clinging to the striped poles of the roundabouts, spinning round and round on painted horses.

The field seemed small, bounded by trees and cottages and the red brick paper shop; a handkerchief of grass laid out under the wet sky, dragged in the centre by two machines that stamped and whirled and flung fragile boats above the earth.

In the light nothing was exciting; even Frances felt this as she climbed slowly on to the roundabout, gazing flatly about her, waiting for the horses to move. When they did, causing her to lurch forward and cling tightly to the pole, she did not scream, only made a little soft 'Oh!' of surprise.

Harriet and I did not want to do anything yet, meaning to save our money till we had taken Frances home and it was almost dark in the field. It was irritating to have to stand there and be seen bedraggled in the rain.

I had tried to explain to my mother that it was awful to go so early; that one looked so silly when the field was full of small children. I could not explain that when it was dark a new dignity would transform the fair into an oasis of excitement, so that it became a place of mystery and delight; peopled with soldiers from the camp and orange-faced girls wearing head scarves, who in strange regimented lines would sway back and forth across the field, facing each other defiantly, exchanging no words, bright-eyed under the needle stars. I

49

could not explain how all at once the lines would meet and mingle performing a complicated rite of selection; orange girls and soldier boys pairing off slowly to drift to the far end of the field and struggle under the hedges filled with blackberries.

It was then that Harriet and I would ride the roundabouts, whirling in the middle of the field and scattering screams into distant corners of the fairground, hearing in our voices the exhausted cries of those others, smearing mouths together in the rain.

Frances climbed politely down and stood unsteadily on the grass. She waved her arms windmill fashion in exaggeration. 'I feel so dizzy.'

'What would you like to do now?' Harriet asked her. 'The same thing again or those dive-bombers?'

Frances looked reflectively at the yellow boats, tethered on steel rods one above the other. They rose slowly crabwise, plunged sickeningly, spun above the grass and climbed again.

'I don't think so.' She moved her shoe in the damp soil and turned her face away from us.

'I'll come with you.' I held out my hand and led her to the pay stool. I felt sad for her disappointment, her inability to enjoy herself after all. The excitement of the fair she had imagined, had not materialised; she was thrown in on herself, politely going through the motions of wonder.

I clutched her arm tightly in the dive-bomber, enacting fear, screaming as we heeled to the ground, heads hanging above the blurred field.

She began to laugh now and when it was all over begged me to stay for another turn, excitedly jumping in her seat, saying, 'Do let's have another ride. Isn't it awful?'

The machine quivered, the tune of *Soldiers of the Queen* marched strongly out from the loudspeaker and lifted us into the sky. I could not be sure that Frances was really excited, or whether, just as I pretended for her sake, so she too laughed and struggled in an effort to please. Perhaps I had spoilt her joy the day before in the garden, when I had said I did not wish to take her.

So together in mutual deceit we plummeted and screamed, breathless at the end, and stumbling a little in the field.

It was growing darker above the spread-eagled trees; multi-coloured lights began to flicker along the Hoop-la stall. A string of pearls, slung from the top of the dynamo van to the roof of the roundabouts, glowed palely against the sky.

I wished for Frances she should go home laden with presents such as one read about in books; traditional prizes of dolls with real golden hair, and little dogs, and a box of chocolates for Mother. But we won nothing, and if we had, the prizes were of such a practical, utility nature we would have been ashamed to carry them. Finally, we bought her a stick of candy floss, that waved loosely before her mouth like fine mist, and took her home.

Mother opened wide arms to Frances, making little sounds of disapproval when she felt the damp hair, fetching a towel immediately from the bathroom to rub protectively the child's head.

It was warm in the front-room with the curtains drawn, and the flowers cast spiked shadows on the tablecloth. My father leaned backwards in his chair, gazing at us through spectacles bandaged firmly at the bridge with sticking plaster.

Almost I wanted to stay with them, not go out riotously into the fairground with Harriet.

I bent to kiss my father on the forehead. I turned to embrace my mother but she was locked in love with Frances so I was embarrassed.

'I won't be late,' I promised them all, opening the door thankfully and walking down the hall.

'Put this on.' My father stood behind me holding a scarf in his hands. He wrapped it round my neck, searching my face with pathetic eyes. He too was afraid and uncertain how to guide me. His face in his inability to pass on experience was crumpled and pompous. I ran out to join Harriet at the gate, the scarf chafing my neck.

It was very cold now; the wind that blew from the sea swept away the fairground music in confusion, so that sometimes we heard it loudly almost in our faces, and then far away and small above the houses.

The field was dark with people; clusters of soldiers like worker-bees rose and fell on the undulating floor of the round-about. The girls linked arm-in-arm, mouths like purple flowers in the artificial light, walked a sedate palais glide for attention. A voice magnified by a loudspeaker sang, 'Your mother was crying, your father was crying and I was crying too'. It should have been funny to hear, but there was such a soaring swooning constancy in the voice, and such a surge of power flooded into the field and overwhelmed the wind, that it assumed tragic proportions.

We rode the roundabouts, shrieking among the painted horses, riding endlessly round and round, waiting for the Tsar to come. When he did come and Harriet shouted to me, 'He's here, Sister Ann,' I did not recognise him, so strangely the light distorted his face.

I stared at the hunch-backed dwarf he had become, his brow like a pale dome, the smile that twisted the black mouth utterly mocking and changed. When he moved to meet us, he bulged hideously under the chain of pearls, his raincoat flapping shroudlike in the wind.

'Hallo,' he said, the cold eyes watching my face carefully.

Harriet wandered away leaving me alone with him.

We both felt it was all so unusual, to be walking together so dangerously in a merry-go-round world, and nothing must be missed. The Tsar won a glass butter-dish at the Hoop-la stall, and put it in his pocket with great satisfaction, smiling at me complacently.

We walked down the field, further into the darkness; at our feet in the wet grass, among the old tins and rubbish, lay the reflections of lights, fragments of glass in blue and yellow and orange, not big enough or tangible enough to take home and look through later, turning the world to gold.

A row of girls went gaily by, heads bent against the rain, flower mouths slightly parted, delicate legs prancing over the puddles. Then there was no one in the whole field but ourselves, walking away down the avenue of bold little lights, walking in desolation. Going over the grass with no one to call us securely in to supper, we became abstracted. No great voice called out terribly, 'Come back, stop!' No great wind came behind us and tore us apart. In a silence bordered by the sad whine of the voice singing wearily now above the soughing trees, the old man kissed my lips, laying them against his own quite flatly and coldly.

Then we walked back towards all the noise and confusion; neither lingeringly nor tenderly, but briskly.

I did not know what to make of it. I had not been kissed many times, but Paul Ricotti had almost swallowed me in his mouth, and the lorry driver Harriet and I had met once when on a picnic had bent me over backwards in his emotion. Both occasions had been funny; the dry calculated embrace of the Tsar might almost have been given by my father, except that it was so sad.

I looked for Harriet among the crowd and found her near the Hoop-la stall, swaying on her feet, her arm round the waist of a soldier.

'Harriet, it's awfully late, please come home.' I felt tired and cold now. The face she turned to me was so wild under the coloured lights I was unable to return her gaze.

Once a long time ago we had met the gardener in the Rhododendron Lands; he had told us we were trespassing and demanded our names and addresses. Harriet, her face illuminated from within by an almost diabolic emotion, had cursed him terribly, walking away a little between the bushes as if to avoid contact with him, white-faced with passion, shouting out insults. The man, appalled by her mood, had turned to me pitifully.

'I'm only doing my job, missie. It's only what's expected of me.'

Harriet trembled on the path and shouted harshly, 'Don't talk to him. Don't talk to the swine.'

Going home she was perfectly controlled and seemed to have forgotten the whole incident.

53

So now I stood hesitatingly, unable to plead with her, fearing her inner exultation. Though she seemed younger than I, it was never my part to be responsible for her; she it was who always decided our actions, and told me what to write in the diary.

I turned and walked out of the field, hoping she would follow.

The Tsar was nowhere in the lane, and though I loitered for a while by the paper shop neither he nor Harriet came.

All the enjoyment had receded from me; I walked miserably down the lane, struggling with a feeling of guilt. There was nothing tangible I had done that was wrong, no sin that I had not committed many times before. I had not even told lies to my parents. I had gone out with their blessing; the scarf now damp and heavy about my neck was proof of this. Still the niggling feeling of uneasiness persisted. I quickened my steps half expecting my father to be at the bend of the road, flurried and harsh with worry at my returning so late.

But there was no one in the lane and, once indoors out of the darkness, my mother and father received me kindly and absent-mindedly, only frowning a little at my wet clothes and exhausted face.

I sat drinking hot milk by the kitchen fire, thinking of Harriet and the Tsar still whirling in infinite darkness outside the window.

8

THE next morning, almost as soon as I had finished breakfast, I heard Harriet whistling outside in the lane.

My mother said firmly, as I dried the dishes, 'You're not going out till I've been helped a little first. She is a nuisance.' I felt disloyal to both of them. 'She's always calling. I've hardly seen you at all this holiday.'

As soon as I could I ran to the door and looked into the garden. Harriet was patiently leaning against the gate, resting her head on its wooden top, swaying backwards and forwards.

'Harriet,' I shouted, 'I'll see you at the library in an hour. Go away now.'

The day was clear and calm, showing no trace of the wildness of last night; between sedate gardens hedged with blossom Harriet went her quiet way, clad in a blue dress and cardigan.

All along the street of shops people called out to me enquiringly, expressing their opinions on my height and weight. I was extremely polite, voice like a bell ringing the changes, weaving my ponderous papal way to the library.

Harriet said in surprise, 'You're so horribly nice and well-mannered. Fancy even speaking to that awful Heatherlee woman after what she said about the Jews.'

'It's all right.' I felt embarrassed. 'It makes things easier in the long run. Diplomacy, you know.'

It was not true; though I spoke graciously to everyone it was Harriet they genuinely liked. Even Mrs Heatherlee, who in conversation called her 'That Dreadful Child', had given her chocolate in the grocer's.

Harriet had once told the station porter Disraeli that on Victory Day Mrs Heatherlee had seven loose women in the backyard; she had heard them gambolling round the coal shed shouting, 'Dear ole Freddie.' Mrs Heatherlee's daughter Margaret had been standing on the platform a few yards away; but even she lent Harriet a book called 'The Dimsie Omnibus'.

'What happened to the Dimsie Omnibus?' said Harriet suddenly, linking up logically that occasion with the smart Mrs Heatherlee now burrowing mole-like into her little black car.

'You burnt it,' I said crossly and entered the library.

'Guess who I met last night?'

'Charlie Chester.'

'Seriously,' said Harriet. 'I came out of the field with the soldier shortly after you left, and Mrs Biggs was standing on the pavement. Dreadfully wet, with no hat and grey hair to her shoulders, waiting for the Tsar.'

'What did she say?' I remembered that Harriet did not yet know he had kissed me.

'Oh, Hallo, almost as if she were at the races. Trying to pretend she always stood on the pavement on rainy evenings. I felt sorry for her so I told her I had seen the Tsar a moment ago in the field. And she said, "Yes I know, he's forgotten something." I nearly said, "You", but walked away with my soldier instead. Do you know he wanted me to take his pay book and address if only I'd go into the bushes with him. In all that rain. They are funny.'

'Harriet!' A feeling of panic and despair had abruptly taken hold of me. 'Please.'

She looked at my face in bewilderment, unable to comprehend immediately.

'Don't,' she said softly, thrusting a book into my hand, standing huddled against me, screening my body.

Tears ran weakly down my cheeks; I ached with the suppressed desire to howl like an animal in pain, deep alleviating moans that would ease me. I stood there mutely, crying endlessly in distress, without knowing why.

Harriet looked down the avenue of shelves. 'Try to stop. Someone might come in.'

I did not care but I tried to stop for her sake, rubbing my hand convulsively across my eyes.

We walked out of the library, Harriet shielding my ravaged face, talking loudly and quickly. We did not stop till we reached the deserted park; until we sat down in the long grass by the public lavatories.

'Why,' said Harriet, 'what happened last night?'

'He kissed me.' My voice was thick and muffled; it sounded very serious and impressive, but what I said seemed trite.

'Well!'

'I just felt sad suddenly, that's all. Her standing in the rain, and you with a soldier, and me in bed, and the Tsar lost without any of us.'

'Oh!' Harriet sounded aggrieved, pulling the grass with irritated fingers, stabbing the dry soil beneath.

'I don't see what there is to cry about,' she added. 'Unless you just feel emotional.'

Though it was not true, I almost felt that this time she had failed to understand; that her experience and mine had not advanced to the same point.

'It's sad,' said Harriet, 'but not as sad as all that. If he likes to amuse himself with you and she likes to follow him and make herself miserable, that's their stupidity. It's sad too, of course, but it's better than nothing for both of them.'

The word 'amuse' caused me intense sorrow. Tears of self-pity welled in my eyes, the park swam in a huge bubble of moisture; I began to cry noisily.

'Don't be illogical,' Harriet spoke sharply.

'It never has been easy, you ought to know by now. In Wales . . .' She was silent suddenly.

'If you really loved him, really and truly.' I sat up angrily, remembering the page in the diary I had not been allowed to read. 'You couldn't possibly go off with anyone else. That's sad too.'

Harriet turned to me in amazement and disbelief.

57

'I didn't love him. I never said I did. You are a fool. And that's sadder than anything else I've ever known.'

Face scornful, she stood up and folded her arms, looking down at me with derision.

I began to feel better. Anger bestowed by Harriet was always more exhilarating than sympathy, and the fact that she had not after all loved the boy in Wales was a thing of happiness in itself. I wiped my face with the hem of my dress and said cheerfully, 'You are quite right, I was just feeling emotional. I feel fine now.'

She was thoughtful going home; she spoke little, a frown of concentration puckered her eyes. I might have thought the sun too strong the way she frowned, but I knew her too well to be so easily mistaken. Outside my gate she paused. Her fingers exploring the blistered paintwork, she said, 'Could you be outside my house a little after nine? I have a plan.'

I felt it was rather late to be going adventuring, and told her so.

'Please yourself,' she said, opening wide eyes with apparent lack of interest.

That evening, some minutes to nine, I was waiting outside her house, sitting on the kerb of the pavement, feeling quite warm and comfortable, not wondering or even curious, just waiting for Harriet. Everything in the lane was so quiet, and similar, so conducive to calmness; the row of red-bricked, identical little houses; a toy-town line of chimney stacks bobbing blackened corks into the colourless sky. A Sunday decorum enveloped the lane in silence and respectability. Behind lace curtains, families sat in mettlesome companionship, shut securely in their boxes on the squares of lawn.

When Harriet appeared the peace of the evening seemed destroyed; she danced with fearful energy on the pavement, eyes bemused and restless, a figure that jerked and pranced with impatience before me.

'It's not quite dark enough yet,' she said, still for a moment looking up at the sky.

Undecided, she waited, then pulled me to my feet, shaking

me till I cried protestingly, 'Stop it, Harriet, you're hurting me.'

She held tight to my arm, face close to mine, the light eyes full-irised, speckled with brown, mouth moistly parted, pellet teeth strained together; then abruptly she released me and walked rapidly down the road. I had to run to keep up with her, for she strode out manfully past the green painted gates and the rubber green hedges, the hem of her dress swinging high above her knees casting shadows on the brittle legs beneath.

She slackened her pace as we turned into Timothy Street and we walked slowly down the road. A confused image of leaf-dappled kerb-stone and diamond-paned windows reflecting light; high ragged fences of yellowed privet and a long avenue of grey houses with tall trees rustling against their walls.

Outside the high black gate Harriet paused, reflected, and walked on to the path that ran beside the house. There was a ditch on one side, the wooden fence of the Tsar's house on the other, and a field at the end. In the field we moved silently along the back of the garden, and paused again outside a smaller gate. Harriet pushed it open cautiously, stepped inside, and turned unsmiling to watch me. I could not move; all was quiet in the field, the back fences of the Timothy Street houses stretched in an unending stockade across the grass. Grey walls rose up behind the enclosure, curtains like eyelids drooped across blackened windows.

Already it was growing darker as I entered the garden, leaving the gate open for a quick return. Narrow and long lay the garden behind the house, spotted with fruit trees and blackcurrant bushes. A bed of flowering cabbages reared monstrous heads, swollen and decayed above the yellow soil. No sound anywhere, the house motionless at the end of the garden, kitchen window small and clouded.

If we're caught, I told myself, we'll say that we kicked a ball into here; if we're caught, we'll say that. If we're caught.

Lights began to glow along the faces of the houses. We cast

huge shadows on the grass, moving nearer and nearer to the Tsar's house. Harriet's shadow stretched further, bent double and dissolved into the wall. We were on a concrete strip before the back door now, and still there was no sound.

'We'll go along the side path to the front garden when it's dark,' whispered Harriet.

We stayed huddled against the wall, breathing softly; my throat felt constricted, I was afraid I would laugh. We waited for a long time. The darkness settled on the field and garden, rolled towards us along an avenue of trees and grass; we waited at the end of the tunnel, hands spread out against the walls patiently.

Harriet moved in the darkness and touched my arm.

'Now,' she said, and on tip-toe we crept along the side wall to the front of the house. Light shone into the garden, voices murmured in the front-room and we waited outside the triangle of orange light. They ought to pull the curtains, I thought. They ought to pull the curtains. We heard distinctly the Tsar say, 'No, thank you,' and the sound of dishes moved.

Then the curtains were drawn across the windows, a thin ribbon of light raddled the grass, a long pinpoint splitting the darkness. Harriet moved to the far window, breaking the knife-edge of light as she crossed the lawn.

I stayed where I was, hoping Harriet would hurry and tell me we could go home. I heard a low hissing noise that seemed to fill the garden, and moved towards her contorted with fear.

'Be quiet, they'll hear you.'

She stood face to the window, peering through a slit in the join of the curtain. I looked through the glass. Directly opposite sat Mrs Biggs, her eyes turned towards me, mouth opening and closing soundlessly. I ducked quickly, dragging Harriet down by the waist.

'She saw me. She saw me.'

'She couldn't have.'

Harriet pulled herself away and looked through the glass once more. I pressed my head against the rough wall, shaken by the image of Mrs Biggs behind the window, heavy body upright in her chair, eyebrows raised questioningly, staring at me. Oh God please, Harriet, hurry, oh God please. Harriet bent towards me.

'Do look. It's perfectly safe.'

'Please, Harriet, come away.'

'Fool! Look at them.'

Reluctantly I took her position, and searched the room. Mrs Biggs leaned over the radio, hips encased in grey tweed. The Tsar was on the sofa, his face hidden behind a newspaper, legs crossed elegantly, small foot swinging. He put down the paper and shook his head. The face was tired and worn, mouth drooping petulantly, skin puckered despairingly beneath his eyes.

I felt Harriet's breath sweep warmly over my neck. She leaned on me heavily, holding my arm. Mrs Biggs crossed the room and sat on the sofa with the Tsar. Suspended in an arc of light, as if posing for posterity, they sat on the sofa staring into the garden; the Tsar jogged one foot up and down gently, hands slack on his thighs. I wondered at the serenity of them both, the relationship that set them a little apart, among furniture they had chosen together. Mrs Biggs moved closer to the Tsar, eyes still turned to the fire, and leaned her grey head on his shoulder. He seemed to wither, the body slumped down, he raised an expressionless face to the ceiling, the fold of skin tightening under his jaw.

Mrs Biggs in time to the music began to stroke his knee with her plump white hand, her head sinking lower on his arm, eyes closed against the light. She opened her mouth but we could not hear what she said, and the Tsar shifted in his seat and spoke to her. Mrs Biggs stood up suddenly, and Harriet pulled me down on to the flower-bed beneath the window. We breathed deeply in fear, kneeling on damp soil.

When we looked again the room was lit by firelight alone. It flickered on the brown wall opposite; the brass fender shone at one point like a star, but the sofa was in deep shadow.

'What's happened?' whispered Harriet. 'Can you see them?'

At that moment a black confused mass heaved and bulged

into the firelight. A grey head snuffed itself against the arm of the couch. Two legs thrashed the air. A hand, round and full, clutched at the edge of the carpet.

I felt huge and bloated with excitement; legs, arms, stomach, mind, ballooned out into the darkness.

The fire blazed up suddenly in the grate; flames thrust outwards into the dark room, illuminating the couch. Under the monstrous flesh of Mrs Biggs, the Tsar lay pinned like a moth on the sofa, bony knees splitting the air, thighs splayed out to take her awful weight. I could not breath. Wave upon wave of fear and joy swept over me.

Like an oiled snake, deep delving and twisting, Mrs Biggs poisoned him slowly, rearing and stabbing him convulsively. Her body writhed gently and was still. Ignoring the woman above him the grey Tsar lay as if dead, pinioned limply, eyes wide and staring, speared in an act of contrition. Full-blown love eddied from the woman, blowzy hips sunk in weariness, litmus flesh soaking up virtue from the body beneath.

Never never never, beat my heart in the garden, never never; battering against invisible doors that sent agonised pains along my wrists, unshed tears dissolving in my head, I crouched against the window helplessly, unable to move.

After a long, long time the light was switched on in the room; the Tsar poured himself a drink, standing with his back to the window. Mrs Biggs in the armchair by the fire held a magazine on her lap, moving her lips as she read, sandalled feet planted firmly on the carpet. Everything was the same; fire burning steadily, light in a pool about the sofa and table, flowers on the mantelpiece. No change in the woman's sensible face, no transfiguration of joy or bliss, and the eyes the Tsar turned to the window as he moved to the fireside were empty and dry.

'It won't do,' said Harriet.

Her voice was too loud in the garden. I turned in fear.

'Let's go now, Harriet.'

Even as I spoke she raised her hand and rapped on the pane of glass. I ran quickly over the lawn and down the path alongside the house. I felt envy as I stumbled through the long grass. I was envious because, though I had felt sickened by what I had seen, I had not dared to voice a protest. No matter how moved or desperate I became I could never do what she had done. My mind could flood with dreams of fighting against stupidity and evil, but it was Harriet who would realise them.

Behind me feet sped down the garden, voices cried out as Harriet lunged against me, light opened up the lawn. As she ran ahead she made strange stifled sounds in her throat; uncontrolled laughter shattered the darkness. It was like a nightmare, the panic-stricken flight into the field, the commanding voice of Mrs Biggs behind us, the swift rush of night air, the fruit trees looming large and formidable in the flood of light, and the sound of laughter far ahead. I whimpered as I ran, breathing promises to God to let me go. Just this once, I promised, oh just this once.

It was no use escaping by the side path into the street, the Tsar would be standing there ready for me. I had to run on into the darkness of the field. I could no longer hear Harriet, for all I knew she had deliberately gone to meet the Tsar.

My body arched and thundered over the ground, excitement carrying me further into the darkness. Each step jarred my body painfully, my heart thudded in my breast till I thought it would break in consequence. Exhausted I fell face downwards in the grass.

Gradually it became quiet and still in the field, my breath ceased to fill the world with noise. I was aware of rustlings in the grass, ringed ploplets of water circling in the ditch; the soft rush of a bird in alarm as it left the dark hedgerow. I knelt upright and looked back towards Timothy Street. Two trees that grew thinly in the earth midway between the houses and the hollow where I lay, splintered the light that shone from the windows, dividing and subdividing each pane of orange glass, so that the whole row of houses moved and shimmered with myriad points of light. A precise clapping sound began behind my head, and turning, I saw a train flickering along the horizon, compartments sending a small glow into the darkness, illuminating the wooden posts beside the railway line. Though it was so late and I knew my parents would be anxious and angry, I could not feel alarmed. The train moved compactly on; a red rear light trailed into the night; the sound of wheels grew fainter in the distance and dissolved away.

If I never went home again, but stayed here in the grass till I died of starvation, that would solve everything. I felt this sincerely and felt unhappy, but I still wanted to laugh. The humour of the situation grew. I dreamed a scene between the doctor and myself.

'But you were very close to death, my dear. Why did you just lie there?'

'Because I saw Mrs Biggs and the Tsar on the couch.'

The doctor turned a critical face to my mother suffering at the end of the bed.

'She is still delirious. A severe shock you know.'

The fantasy unfolded in my brain, tentative shoots probed crabwise into the recesses of the night; figures with lanterns stumbled over my body, the child's chest rising shallowly, body slender at last in near death, lips murmuring in delirium . . . I saw Mrs Biggs and the Tsar on the couch.

When Harriet all but trod on me I screamed sharply with shock. 'It's me,' she said. 'It's terribly late.'

'It would be better not to go home at all now,' I said unable to see her face in the darkness. Harriet thought about it.

'It would be lovely in the woods. Quite warm too. But we'd have to go home in the morning, and then what would we say?' I imagined sleeping on the floor of warm leaf mould under the branches, wind blowing in from the sea, a murmur of incoming tide more vast than by day. A sinister insidious sound of water stretching along the coast, enveloping slowly the broad sands.

'We'll have to go now,' said Harriet.

The nearer we came to the lane the slower we walked. Even Harriet was alarmed at the lateness of the hour, afraid of her predictable father. At the gate of my house Mother waited in

64

a flurry of anger. Inside the house my fear evaporated as she spoke sharply to me.

'What do you mean by staying out till this time? How dare you cause us so much worry. Where have you been?'

Each question dissipated a little of her anger. Head bent humbly I did not answer. It was not expected of me. My father had gone to bed very worried. My mother had stopped him phoning the police to say we were missing. Harriet's father had been on the phone twice to see if she was here. It was almost half past eleven . . . Did I know that?

'I'm sorry,' I murmured.

I could go to bed now. In the morning my mother would be cold and distant with me but by afternoon friendly and loving once more. My father would look sullenly at me and bring back sweets when he returned from work. Everything would be the same, tomorrow.

9

I COULD not find my notebook.

We each had a book in which to write down our impressions of people we might meet. I had carried it in the pocket of my school blazer when we visited Timothy Street. I sat helplessly in my bedroom, feeling ill at the implications of such a loss. If I had dropped it in the garden and Mrs Biggs found it, nothing could save me. There was nothing in it because we tore out each page on completion and placed it in the box with the diary. But my address was on the cover for all to read: No. 4 Sea Lane, Formby, Lancs, England, Europe, The World.

Harriet looked grave when I told her, but for once was unable to advise how to act. She sat moodily on the bed, forbidden to go out. Her judicious father had hit her about the head the night before. She said he laid strong palms about her ears, measuring each blow, swearing all the time. 'I shouldn't wonder if I have a father-complex later,' she said. I went with stealth down the stairs to the front door, avoiding her parents successfully, and let myself out into the garden.

I had not missed the notebook till after tea; Mrs Biggs, should she have searched the garden after last night's intrusion, had already had nine hours in which to find it. It was now a little after six, and the Tsar would be home from work. Either I walked to the shore in the hope of a chance meeting, and there appealed to him to find the notebook, or I went alone now to Timothy Street, and searched the garden. Since the night of the fair we had not met, at least to his knowledge, and it was probable he might go out in the hope of seeing me. I could tell him we were playing a joke, that Harriet and I had been in the garden for fun – he need not know we had watched through the curtain – and that I was afraid I had dropped the notebook when we ran away.

The fear that seized me at the thought of Mrs Biggs calling on my mother, left no room for embarrassment at seeing the Tsar. Besides, the scene on the couch had shown the unimaginable to be pitiful; a function as empty of dignity and significance as brushing one's teeth. The darkness had heightened the tension and mystery, but it was Mrs Biggs who had put out the lights. It was her I hated, not the Tsar. Henceforth I could wait, without tarantella nerves, for the Tsar to lay his lips on mine, remembering he had loved Mrs Biggs, times without number, long before I was born.

My mother had said I was to be out for no more than an hour. Supposing they had thought us thieves last night, and Mrs Biggs, nervous, asked the Tsar to stay indoors in deference to her fears. I would only waste time going to the shore. Still I hovered there, outside Harriet's house, unable to make a decision. A figure turned the corner beyond the cottage hospital, walking close to the lemon wall, head bent, hands in pockets. Though I could not see his face I recognised the elegant walk, the fastidious feet pacing the lane. I ran into the garden, consumed with excitement, and whistled under Harriet's window.

'Harriet, Harriet, he's here, he's coming down the lane.'

Harriet disappeared from the open window immediately, and I ran backwards and forwards over the lawn, not daring to peer into the lane in case he saw me, but unable to be calm. When Harriet opened the door I almost knocked her over in my excitement, thrusting her backwards into the hall.

'Harriet, what shall we do? He's in the lane.'

'Shut the door.' She pushed her head under the frilled curtain to watch through the glass. A bird hopped warily over the grass, wings folded close, bright eyes searching the soil.

'Are you sure you saw him?' Harriet turned her bridal veiled head and touched my cheeks with her hand.

'Are you sure you just didn't feel emotional again?'

The bird flew swiftly up into the trees as the Tsar entered the gate. Harriet held my hand firmly and led me into the back room where her parents sat.

'Father,' she said, 'Mr Biggs is coming up the path.'

A neighbourly expression transfused her father's face. A jovial smile softened the mouth habitually severe; he cleared his throat self-consciously.

'Oh, good. I expect he wants to see me. Better put the kettle on, Mother.' Importantly he went out into the hall.

Harriet's mother placed coquettish hands to her hair, patting the waves more securely above her forehead. She was never deliberate in her flirtatiousness, it was more a habit than anything else. Her husband called her his 'little woman', and with all men she was bright and coy. So now she preened herself for the task in hand, bending and plumping the cushions adroitly, straightening the drab table runner, hiding the newspaper behind the wireless. She spoke worriedly to Harriet before going into the kitchen.

'Just sit quiet on the sofa, and don't interrupt your father more than you can help.'

Voices were loud in the hall. The Tsar laughed. I felt there was very little in his life to laugh at, and sat clenching my hands behind my back; nostrils and throat were constricted, a sweet spasm of shuddering gripped and as abruptly left my body, leaving me inert on the sofa. Harriet's mother came out of the kitchen, and greeted the Tsar profusely. He stood in the doorway, bowing slightly, hidden by her body, surrounded by friendliness. Then he straightened and saw Harriet and me on the couch under the window. A moment of indecision, eyes meeting briefly; then he walked boldly to us. Harriet pressed her arm hard against my side; there was a soft rush of air as her mouth opened widely to smile; the pressure of her arm strengthened as if she sensed my growing thoughtlessness. I cared nothing for her warning, nothing for the tableau before me. The man of justice poised by the door, the woman in the act of placing a saucer on the table, seemed to swivel round in the room and become unfocused. I stared with wonder at the Tsar. I felt quite safe. I was there by intent, not accident. I had been put on the sofa by Harriet's mother. None could stop me looking at him, not even Harriet.

She said, 'Hallo, Mr Biggs.'

He sat on the chair beside the table, white shirt against dark suit, city shoes of black leather beating a tattoo against the leg of the table. A thin hand splayed out on his knee, the middle finger stained with nicotine; handkerchief tipping his breast pocket, eyes small in his sallow face. No longer the Tsar of the night of the fair and the father kiss, nor the puppet Tsar on the couch behind curtained windows. A new Tsar of offices and daily work, one who talked business with other men, and carried a brief-case to the city. I watched the adults talking pleasantly and felt marooned with Harriet on the sofa, almost a feeling that I was indeed a child.

Why didn't he have children? Why didn't they make a child out of the nights spent under the beech leaves?

The Tsar was saying, 'So I'm afraid I won't, regrettably, be able to play golf on Saturday.'

'Oh, too bad.' Harriet father's mouth drooped in disappointment at a routine violated. His pleasure at the Tsar's visit soured. He drummed petulant fingers on the arm of the chair. Brightly his wife poured out tea, little finger crooked genteelly, wrist arched with the weight of the pot.

'What a shame, dear, but there's always another day.'

Another day. The notebook lost in the vengeful Mrs Biggs's garden; the impending visit to my mother, face righteous, voice gravely telling the awful story. Childhood fled from me, I sat upright and watched the clock. I would have to leave very soon, my mother would be waiting.

Harriet leaned forward and rested her elbows on her knees, staring at the Tsar with interest.

'Mr Biggs, why did you stop wearing glasses?'

Her mother looked at her and then at the Tsar, her

face expressing the hope that Harriet was not being rude.

The Tsar said, 'I broke so many pairs I just gave up wearing them.'

I felt he was ashamed in front of me at the admission. I wished I knew if I only imagined he cared for me, it seemed so strange the things I attributed to him. I did not know where the dream and the reality merged, I did not know anything.

'I may have to wear glasses soon,' I lied. What was the point of it? What did I mean him to understand? It was seven o'clock and I dare not stay any longer. I hated the bulk of me standing up in the room, clumsily moving to the door, self-consciously saying good night, avoiding their eyes. He stood up when I did, and for a moment I thought he too was taking his departure, but it was only a blessed politeness. Did he stand up for me because he thought me a woman? I beseeched Harriet silently to come to the door with me, but she only rocked gently on the sofa and said casually, 'Good night dear,' and left it to her mother to accompany me into the hall.

For two evenings and two days I waited for Mrs Biggs to ring the bell, and disturb the credulous mind of my mother.

Harriet told me to write in the diary, 'I am waiting now only for Mrs B. to call with the notebook. All the hours pass waiting for the fulfilment of this. I can neither eat nor sleep . . .' I felt this was a little dramatic, but it was true, and no other words seemed to evoke clearly what I was suffering.

On the third day, when still Mrs Biggs had not called, a faint hope filled me. She had found the notebook, but would feel foolish telling my mother, and she was not going to tell her. Harriet agreed this might be so, and told me not to worry.

'It's a closed incident, dear. You must forget it.'

While we still could not go walking in the evening and were restricted to one hour after tea, we spent the time writing in the diary. One passage in particular puzzled me. Harriet dictated, 'If two people commit a sin, it is a bad thing. If one person commits a sin with another, it is worse. The passive one is the person most guilty, and should be punished for betraying himself . . .' Then she made me write, 'Events must be logically concluded. We must be tidy.' When I questioned her about it she was only evasive.

'I'm right,' was all she would say. 'Really I am, trust me.'

'But, Harriet, I feel funny about him.' There was no reply. She lay on her bed and would not look at me.

'Harriet, you know the way you would not let me see what you had written about the boy in Wales?' I tried to sound at ease but it was an appeal.

'Yes.' She was looking at me now.

'Well, I feel that way about the Tsar.'

'What way? What way is that?'

Dare I say it? Even the relationship between us was changing. I ought not to have to explain.

'What on earth are you going on about?'

I spoke self-consciously, running the words together in embarrassment.

> Shall my heart remain my own?
> Oh the tears upon his cheeks;
> Do I dare to walk alone?
>
> How the beech leaves pale and whiten,
> How still the little churchyard lies.
> Let compassion shut my eyes.

'What's that got to do with it?' asked Harriet, but not crossly. 'I wrote that after we met those boys from the remand home when I took my clothes off and you wouldn't because your knickers were filthy.'

'They weren't filthy,' I protested. 'I told you, they were my mum's and they were pink with awful lace.'

'Well, so what?'

'I love Mr Biggs,' I said, and wondered instantly why I had called him that. It sounded so funny – 'I love Mr Biggs'.

Harriet sat up. 'In that case we better hurry. There's not much of the holidays left.'

71

I resented the 'we'. It wasn't we who loved the Tsar, it was I alone.

'But I don't know that I want it to be an experience,' I said miserably. 'I don't think I want it to be something for the diary.'

Harriet spoke in the same reasonable way she talked to her mother.

'At thirteen there is very little you can expect to salvage from loving someone but experience. You'll go back to school for years, you'll wear a gym tunic long after all this is over. What do you expect? No one will let you love yet. You're not expected to. They don't even know how to do it themselves. And all he'll feel for you is a sort of gentle nostalgia. No – bring it to a logical conclusion. If you don't you'll feel emotional for ages over something that was pretty trivial.'

'But what if we find it's not trivial?' I was appalled by the wisdom of us both. It seemed unnatural. Why had I not noticed it before?

'Don't let's suppose,' Harriet said efficiently. 'Now write in the diary what I tell you. "This man is a very complex one. He seems to like to suffer. It is a very great weakness and one that she (the wife) has helped to cultivate. We saw him on the couch in an attitude of resignation, and we thought the wife was to blame. But now we are not so sure of this. We caught a glimpse of their life through the window and we found it disgusting and abasing. He should not submit to a woman like that. Obviously he is a victim and likes to be punished." '

'But we don't know, Harriet, we can't be sure.'

Harriet went on firmly, 'We must work quickly to punish him in a way he will not like.' I wrote it down in my best hand-writing and felt uneasy.

Voices could be heard bouncing in a tight ball against the ceiling. I stopped writing and listened.

'Are they quarrelling?'

'Yes,' said Harriet.

I was interested. Harriet said they often quarrelled and that it was terrible when they did because the little woman began to cry, and the father grew more bullying to protect himself.

'Open the door,' said Harriet, and placed her hands palm downwards against the floorboards, as if to brace herself for an inevitable shock. I did as I was told. Two voices were raised and both were angry and I looked at Harriet inquiringly because I knew the little woman was not given to argument. Harriet shook her head and whispered, 'They can't be quarrelling . . . unless they're both angry about the same thing.'

We tried hard to hear what it was they said, tried to piece words together but it was difficult, until suddenly the father clearly said, 'Right!', and the door below opened and his voice shouted fearfully loud, 'Harriet, come here!'

Harriet did not move. She stared at me with wide eyes, mouth open, unable to breathe.

'Harriet, do you hear?'

Harriet got to her feet and crept over to the window. She cupped her hand over her mouth and called, 'What is it?'

The hand over her mouth made it seem as if the bedroom door was shut and she had not heard properly. She motioned me frantically with extravagant hands to close the door. The father below called once more.

'Come down!'

All was quiet; the parents waited in the silence. Harriet leaned against the window, she pressed her nose to the glass.

'You'll have to go.'

I was frightened that the father would come upstairs and fetch her.

'All right, all right,' said Harriet sullenly. She kicked with her foot at the skirting-board and hunched her shoulders. Moving to the door, her face in shadow, she passed me humilated. Before she had reached the bottom of the narrow stairs the voice called,

'Both of you, please.'

Harriet looked up at me to where I stood on the landing and stared at me. I could not be sure whether she wanted me to walk downstairs and out of the house and defy her father, slamming the door loudly and whistling easily as I shut the gate behind me. I just followed her down the steps and entered the living-room.

Her father sat with deception in his chair by the fire, pushing his feet against the fender, easing his toes more surely into his brown slippers. The little woman with despairing face stood with her back to the fire, and touched her cheek with one hand as if to reassure herself.

'Now,' said her father, smiling pleasantly at me, 'I'm just going to ask a plain question and I want a plain answer. None of your clever talk, Harriet, do you understand?'

He gave a vicious little toss of his head and turned to her. If Harriet understood she gave no sign, but stood looking out of the window into the dark shrouded garden. Her mother leaned forward to poke the fire unnecessarily and a live coal fell into the brown-tiled hearth. He looked at her with distaste at this and pouted his lips bad-temperedly. The noise irritated his already inflamed nerves.

'What were you doing round at Mr Biggs's house the other night?'

At once my mind turned and spun out intricate patterns of invention. I had felt faint as we passed the Tsar's house and Harriet had dragged me on to the grass. We had banged the window to get help . . . because I needed help. I was always feeling faint; I was ill. I had not felt well for a long time now; the doctor thought I was growing too fast. Harriet was saying, 'We went a walk. We felt like an apple so we went into the garden.'

She bent down over the back of the empty rocking chair, swaying forward with it, letting her plaits hang down to brush against the green cushion. Her mother swept industriously at the ash in the hearth, flushed with the heat from the fire. She tightened her grip on the brittle brass rod of the ornamental brush, waiting for the blow to fall.

'I see. You went to pick apples.' Her father leaned back, smiling now, his hands touching only at the tips of his fingers, as if in delicate prayer. 'And what else did you do beside picking apples?'

'What do you mean? We ate the apples . . . why?'

'Perhaps you remember what else you did, eh?' He looked at me over his hands and waited.

'Well we just . . . I mean we looked at the window. We didn't do much, honestly.'

I had betrayed myself and Harriet. I had appealed to the man. I had defended myself involuntarily by the use of the word 'honestly'. Harriet stopped rocking the chair and hung motionless, head down.

'Well, I won't have it, do you hear. I won't have it.' Blood suffused his face; an angry vein throbbed in his temple.

'Your mother had a visit from Mrs Biggs today. She said you spied on them through the window. She doesn't like it, do you hear?'

Harriet stared at her father. 'How did she know we looked through the window?'

'Because she did. I'm asking the questions.' His voice strengthened. He seemed to be filling himself with air, ready to blast us from the room.

He began to bully Harriet in earnest. He shouted with eyes dark with emotion. Her mother and I stayed as grieved on-lookers, relieved to be watching. As Harriet remained silent, he became threatening. The more he shouted and lost control, the more difficult became his position, and as yet he could not say why it was so wrong of us to spy through the window. Naughty, yes, but not wicked.

He was afraid of what Harriet might say in reply. He was afraid even now she would ask him, and he shouted rather to drown her question should it come, than because he was righteously angry. I began to feel sorry for him. Harriet was so strong in battle; even I was strong. He had not the courage to tell her what worried him, that we were young girls, that the Tsar was a funny fellow, wandering down to the shore on his own, that there had been incidents in the past never properly explained, involving Harriet and men. Instead he said that we mustn't go round to the house any more, that we had to be indoors earlier, that it was about time we realised we were

75

growing up. At this Harriet permitted herself a small smile, and looked down at the carpet with pretended amusement. Finally she said:

'But what is so awful about peeping through Mr Biggs's window, Father?'

It was very cruel. He threw himself forward in his seat and glared at her. His hands gripped the arms of his chair furiously and impotently. He was choking with the hurt and fear he felt, and his round blue eyes stared for a moment at Harriet as if she were a landscape utterly barren, distorted by lightning and unknown. Then he said brokenly, 'Good God, girl!' He got up and stood broadly over her as if to make her fall down, overpowered by the bulk of him, but Harriet mercilessly looked up at him, eyebrows arched inquiringly.

'You talk to her.' He turned to her mother. 'I'm through, blast her. Let her go to the devil.'

He went to the door, and as he moved his slipper came off his left foot, and rather than return and struggle into it he kicked it away from him and slammed the door. He shouted all the way upstairs; we could hear him repeating endlessly that he was through, through, until the bedroom door closed on him. The slipper stood on end against the far wall, shabby and badly out of shape.

While her father was in the room, Harriet had seemed the victor. Now that he lay muttering on his bed upstairs, chanting that he was through, all through, we felt guilty and deflated. Harriet leaned her head dejectedly against the mantelpiece. She said to her white-faced mother:

'What have we done wrong, little woman? Why did he go on like that?'

I knew that Harriet was upset because the little woman had been exposed to the scene, that she wanted to comfort her.

'I think you're extremely unkind, Harriet.'

Her mother spoke formally in front of me.

'You know why you shouldn't go round to Mr Biggs's house, especially not in their garden, looking through their window. It's not nice behaviour . . . He just doesn't want you to do anything you'll regret . . . He's so proud of you and you do everything you can to antagonise him.'

'Well, you shouldn't have told him. You know how stupid he is.'

The muttering upstairs broke out afresh.

'Put the wireless on, dear.'

Her mother was so resigned and kind it was awful. Harriet turned on the wireless to drown the sound of her father's voice, in case the neighbours should hear. I knew this because Harriet had told me that when she came home from school and the wireless was on, she knew there had been trouble and her father was in a temper. I wondered if along the whole row of houses and back rooms the wireless hummed out its message. Her mother hated the wireless at other times and refused to have it switched on. Cheerful dance-music filled the room. It might have been a holiday the way the tune spun and spiralled among us.

Her mother continued, 'For Heaven's sake, dear, try to see it from his point of view for a change.' The little woman warmed to her task and became almost coherent. 'If you don't mind about him at least consider me a little. It's not you that bears the brunt of it. He'll be in a mood for days. I can't stand it. You know how low it makes me.'

'All right, all right.' Harriet sounded desperate.

After a pause her mother said, 'I did say to Mrs Biggs that she could not expect me to believe such an extraordinary tale without some sort of proof. I did say that.'

It was strange. The little woman sought to justify herself to us.

'What extraordinary tale?' asked Harriet gently, as if dealing with a child unable to tell right from wrong. 'What did she tell you?'

'She said you were in her garden the other night, the front garden, and that you knocked on the window and swore at them, and ran away. Were you in the garden?'

I waited for Harriet to answer. I would have denied it utterly but; as I expected, she said in the same gentle tone,

'Yes, we were. I did knock on the window. I said damn you, but I wasn't swearing.'

Harriet's mother sat in the armchair, not knowing what to say.

'But why?' she asked finally. 'What on earth possessed you to do such a wicked thing?'

Harriet smiled indulgently. 'It wasn't wicked, little woman, it was a joke.'

I felt admiration for the way she spoke, the calm refusal to be blackmailed into submissiveness by parental grief. Where I would have broken down and begged for forgiveness, Harriet reasoned sensibly.

'Who told Mrs Biggs it was us?' she asked. 'Did she recognise my voice?'

'Mr Biggs caught a glimpse of your face, and persuaded Mrs Biggs not to inform the police. He also found this in the garden next morning.'

The notebook lay on the sideboard face down.

'I see,' said Harriet, picking up the book and handing it to me.

I took it, and held it to me guiltily.

Harriet's mother looked at me. 'I don't suppose,' she said cruelly, 'your mother would be very proud of the episode.'

Only the fact that Harriet was in the room stopped me from going down on my knees and begging her to be lenient.

'No,' I stammered wretchedly, 'I'm sorry.'

Disgusted, Harriet turned away, and there I might have stayed for ever, unable to move from the room, dejected and at a loss in front of her mother, if she had not said to me, 'You'd better run along home, dear.' She hesitated. 'I should be glad, dear, if you didn't say anything at home about tonight – he's not been well you know, dear. He has a lot of trouble with his stomach.'

Harriet cried impatiently, 'Oh stop making excuses. She wouldn't dare mention tonight, and if she did, what does it matter? It's so absurd.'

'You don't think he'll come round to our house do you?'
I could not help myself.

Harriet flung her arms above her head despairingly.

'You two – you're a pair, aren't you? He's not been well you know – it's his stomach – you don't think he'll come to our house?' She mimicked us cruelly, looking down on us with disgust.

I had so much in common with her mother; but she would be comforted by Harriet – after I had gone. Harriet would sit at her feet and put her arms round her and tell her not to take it so hard. I felt ashamed at my selfishness. Poor little woman. How would she go to bed? How could she go into the sulky bedroom and lie down beside the muttering man with his face swollen with anger? Perhaps she would stay by the fire all night with Harriet, discussing me, saying how cowardly and deceitful I was, how stout, how I could never tell the truth. I resolved to go away, not just away to school in a few weeks' time, but away for ever, so that Harriet would be sorry.

'Good night.'

'Good night,' said Harriet grudgingly. 'Better leave it for a day or two. I'll see you on the shore some time.'

'All right.'

I went out of the back door and ran down the path in the dark almost sobbing. I leaned on the cherry tree that grew against the garage and listened to the loud beating of my heart. I rubbed my cheek across the slender trunk of the tree and whispered over and over, 'I can't bear it, I can't, I can't bear it.'

I wanted to see Harriet just once more before I went away. I walked on tip-toe along the path and stood at the side of the window. I was reminded of the night we had spied on the Tsar; it was another thing to remember this long summer by, an endless peering through secret windows.

Harriet's mother sat on her chair by the fire reading the evening paper. The wireless was quite loud and she had put fresh coal in the grate. Her face was screwed up in concentration over the newsprint. Her mouth bulged slightly as she chewed a sweet. Harriet was not there.

I leaned against the wall and thought it over. If you were very unhappy you could not possibly eat sweets. I felt sure I could not. And if Harriet really loved her mother she would be with her; if her mother needed her.

I went round the house to Harriet's room at the front. Her light was on, but the curtains were drawn across the windows. Three people of one flesh, all alone in separate rooms, one chewing sweets and reading the evening paper, one chanting out his tom-tom message of doom, and the third motionless on her bed, dry eyes wide open under the electric light.

It began to rain as I stood there keeping watch over Harriet. That was it, I would stay here all night and never move.

Harriet pulled back the curtains and opened the window. She leaned on the sill and stared out into the garden. I did not know what to do. She wanted to be alone, she was glad I had gone home. I could sense in the shadowed inclination of her head and neck that she fancied herself unseen and solitary. Greatly daring, I whispered, 'Harriet . . . it's me . . . Harriet.'

'What are you doing?'

'I'm going away, Harriet.

'I should hope so. You'll catch your death there . . . it's raining.'

So miserable was I that I had forgotten the rain. How could she be so cruel as to misunderstand?

'I mean I'm going away for good, Harriet.'

In my anxiety to make her understand I stepped on to the flower-bed under her window and peered up at her.

'Oh, you fool,' Harriet half said, half cried. 'And mind the plants. He'll be furious. You're trampling all over them.'

She withdrew into the room and shut the window. The curtains with finality closed once more.

I stood in the rain and wished her in hell.

Victor Sylvester was still conducting foxtrots on the wireless. Bending my neck I stretched out my arm and went quick, quick, slow across the lawn. Then I got down on my knees in the grass and brushed the top soil of the flower-bed in case her father should be furious. I wished I could erase my love for Harriet as easily as my footprints. I spoke seriously to myself on the way home, resolving to be more adult in my emotions. I felt exhausted, as if I had run for miles in a high wind.

10

ON Sunday evening I met Harriet outside the Cottage
Hospital. I had said nothing to my parents who, working
laboriously in the garden, hardly seemed to notice when I
fetched my coat and walked out of the gate. Harriet had telephoned me after tea, and told me she had thought of a good
plan to help me get over my love for the Tsar. I felt that I
did not want to get over it, such a strange mixture of pain and
pleasure it gave me, but I could not tell her so.

As we walked to the woods she told me what she had
decided. First, I must put my meetings with the Tsar on a
more regular basis. No more going down to the sea, as we did
now, in the hope of meeting. I must arrange times and places
with him.

'But, Harriet,' I protested weakly, 'he may not want it.'
The fields along the cinder path swayed in rhythm, as
the wind moved over the tops of grasses. Trees, fields, and
hedges fluttered in one circular regular spasm, and were
still.

'Also you must get him to kiss you again,' said Harriet,
walking steadily, paying no attention to my interruption. It
sounded very simple. I was not afraid of the Tsar any more,
but there was a difference between that and actually thrusting
myself on him. I shook my head and wondered what was
wrong. The woods seemed smaller and blacker, the church
tower breaking through the pines, tiny and ineffectual. Time
was when the whole earth lay buried beneath the blue trees,
and the tower split the clouds with a fist of iron.

'Mrs Biggs usually goes away for a few days in the summer to see her sister,' Harriet was saying. 'You must find out when, and we'll call on the Tsar at his house.'

She had told me before that Mrs Biggs's sister had a backward child. The sister took drugs to stop the child from growing in her, and it tore her body when it slid with monstrous head on to the rubber sheet. That was what Harriet said. Would Mrs Biggs sit listening to Children's Hour, idiot child on her lap?

But Harriet was too serious. It was different from the first evening she had come home from Wales, when we swayed giddily to meet the Tsar waiting under the silver-painted lamppost.

The lane was empty as we turned the corner by the Canon's house; high tunnel of broad elms motionless beneath the sky, the light filtering white and radiant between the still leaves. We climbed the wall into the graveyard and stood ankle deep in the black ivy, creeper stems of wine-red coursing the earth like veins. Pale shoots of beech fluttered against the fence, small leaves fanned out precisely.

'What if he doesn't come?' I asked Harriet, walking away through the tangle of grass and ivy towards the church. She tossed her head, jerking the colourless plaits of hair about her ears, and shouted:

'He will, dear. He must.'

She was always so sure now. As if returned from Wales surging with power and knowledge, she straddled the summer days like a colossus, carrying me with her.

The Canon kept the key of the church under the hair mat in the porch. We used it whenever we liked; sometimes we had picnics when it rained and sat in the pews eating sandwiches, and other times we took refuge there from the streams of city children that screamed and ran about the woods on holidays. The Canon had surprised us once delivering loud sermons from the pulpit, but Harriet had charmed him with her ambition, newly discovered for his benefit, of becoming a missionary and carrying the word of God to foreign lands. He called her the Constant Nymph, lisping the words in his baby-ish voice honeyed with sentimentality.

Harriet bent down and felt for the key under the mat. A fine cloud of white sand puffed out across the stones as the mat flapped back into place. She turned the key in the lock, and pushed the massive door inwards, and stepped inside. Dust spiralled upwards in the sunlight that shone through the stained windows. Harriet stood beside the stone christening font, holding an imaginary baby in her arms.

'I baptize thee in the name of the Father, the Mother, the Tsar,' she chanted, looking to the doorway where I stood, watching my face curiously. I smiled uneasily, feeling unbearably hot in my school coat of navy blue.

'Are we going to wait here? It's so hot, Harriet.'

She joined me at the door, folding brown arms across her chest, and peered into the lane. A man rode by on his bicycle, trilby hat bobbing grotesquely above the church wall. It looked like a distorted bird limping horizontally among the trees. 'Hallo!' he shouted, to someone in the lane.

'It's him,' said Harriet, holding my arm with fierce fingers. 'I'm sure it's him.'

I thought of how Thomas Becket had run into some church, and flung himself across the altar in order to escape the hired assassins, and wanted to do the same; but Harriet held tight to my arm and I could not move. It was awful just to stand there, smiling widely while he walked up the path, anchored together against him. He smiled too from the gate, hands fumbling on the catch, gazing with awkward intensity at the graves bordering the path. He had to smile at us twice, and look away, before he finally reached us.

'Hallo?'

'Hallo, Tsar?'

He whirled his hat between his fingers, avoiding our eyes. I thought he must feel ashamed, creeping away down the lane to meet such cruel friends. It was very difficult to know what to do now. Harriet just stood there in the porch, eyes turned to the sky, ignoring us both.

I said, 'I'm sorry about the other night. It was only a joke.'
I wished I hadn't mentioned it. He might wonder how long we
had watched through the window.

'She was a bit difficult,' he said, watching Harriet almost
humbly. 'I had to tell her it was you. She would have called
the police.'

For a moment I wondered if it was Harriet he loved, the
way he looked at her over my head.

Then he said :

'Harriet, I want to talk to you.'

She turned to look at him, tongue curling out a little beneath
her lips.

'All right.' She spoke to me commandingly. 'Go away, I'll
call you later when we've finished.'

I hoped he would tell me I might remain, but he hardly
glanced at me, hat twirling relentlessly in his hands.

I walked a little way between the graves, and sat down
under the trees with my back to the porch. It was very quiet.
He was telling her he thought me stout and large. He wanted
to tell her what happened on the couch was meaningless. He
was saying, 'She's unintelligent, but you understand,' placing
thankful arms about her neck.

In despair I stood up, trying to be brave. I would stand
behind them mutely. Just this once I would not be afraid. My
eyes would not betray dislike or pain, only a gentle sadness
that would for once outweigh the solid cheerfulness of my
body.

Suddenly Harriet ran out on to the path in front of me. I
stopped in surprise, so quick was the movement. Then I was
filled with disproportionate fear, as if I had lit a match and
dropped it in the grass, seeing in the small flame a whole world
afire before I trod it underfoot. There was such fury in the
headlong flight of her body over the grass that I could not call
out. Astride the wall she turned and faced me accusingly, then
dropped into the lane. I could not be sure whether she was in
earnest or not. It could be that it was an elaborate way of
leaving me alone with the Tsar, and that even now she was

walking calmly and with great satisfaction over the fields towards home.

The porch was empty, the huge door half closed against me.
I called softly, 'Mr Biggs,' pausing for a moment outside. 'Are
you there?' I had to call him Mr Biggs, though it sounded
comical. 'Mr Biggs, Mr Biggs! Is it true that your ribs, are as
thin as the bark on the trees?' Harriet's rhyme jingled sense-
lessly up and down in my brain. The Tsar sat facing the altar,
back bent, head sunk forward on his chest. It would be so
easy to slip out silently into the graveyard, and run thankfully
over the fields. Only the thought of Harriet's anger made me
move hesitatingly towards him. It was like a play I had seen,
where a man had failed terribly in business. The daughter,
home from expensive school, stood helplessly beside him, wishing to touch his arm and tell him she did not care about leaving
school, but frightened of the hopeless face he would turn to her.

'Mr Biggs.'

The face of the Tsar, when he did look at me, was so normal
and ordinarily thoughtful, that I stared at him with disbelief.
I fought the desire to call him Father, and said nervously,
'What was the matter with Harriet?'

'I'm not sure, child. I think I told her the truth.'

'What do you mean?'

'I said she had an evil mind.'

I was appalled. I wanted to shout, 'I love Harriet. She's
brave and true and beautiful,' but the words stuck in my
throat. Instead, I said :

'I don't understand you.'

'I know. You haven't an evil mind.'

It was all so unlike what I had imagined. He was telling me
that I was the good, the wonderful one. Harriet so thin, so
brown in the sun, so like I wanted to be, was the outcast. I
could not love him after all if he hated Harriet. If I loved him
when he thought Harriet evil, then I could not love her. How
could one be evil who walked every day the lane to the sea,
and breathed the air from the pines? And if Harriet was in
truth evil, then I was, and so was the Tsar.

86

'Why is she evil?'

'She'll perhaps tell you herself.'

The sun had gone behind the trees, leaving the church dark and no longer warm; the rows of pews rose up out of the stone floor like the headstones in the graveyard outside. The Tsar made no move, but sat there gently rubbing his hands, warming himself.

I began to grow tired of the scene.

'I had better go now,' I said, staring down the church to the altar now in shadow. He did not move in his seat, only bowed his head as if in acquiescence, and then suddenly, belatedly,

'Don't go.'

I fidgeted unhappily, scraping my nails along the polished wood by his head, unsure of what I should do.

'Why?' I said. I meant it to be knowledgable and flirtatious, the way Harriet's mother used it, but it sounded childish, a cry in the dark.

'Why?' he said, mimicking my voice unkindly, petulantly mouthing the word. My eyes filled with tears. I swallowed quickly, wondering if he disliked me. The tears were not for that reason; it was the darkness and the lost echoes of our voices in the darkness, and the black shapes of trees outside the high windows, that made me want to cry. If I creased my face upwards in a grief-stricken smile, and wailed between clenched teeth a long-drawn-out wail of sadness down the church, then I could cry. As it was I could only stand there silently, the tears unshed and almost gone. If he did not want me to go, why did he not talk to me, or at least look at me? In this dim light shadows would create wonders in my round, full face. I imagined I looked pale and ethereal, hair smudged about my head, eyes shining with faint tears.

When he did look at me, and said softly in his amused dry voice, 'What a tragic little Muse,' it was almost as if I sat bare-footed in the sand, hearing the Italian say 'Dirty little Angel'.

What was a Muse? A thoughtful person, or a Greek goddess singing siren songs on the rocks above the sea? It was a beautiful, beautiful word. 'What a tragic little Muse,' I told Harriet tenderly, in my mind.

It was so clumsy an action when he stood up and placed his arms round me, that I had to close my eyes tight and cling to the words to keep the beauty there.

'Please,' I said unhappily, hating the sour smell of skin against my cheek. 'Please let me go.'

He dropped his arms at once, standing back and smoothing his hair in a gesture of weariness. It was so dark I could not see his face clearly, only the outline of his hand placating the thin hair. I began to feel light-hearted and sure of myself, saying over and over again, 'I'm sure it's terribly late. I'm sure it is. It must be terribly late, Tsar.'

Anxious and relieved to be going I pulled at the big door, now closed against the churchyard. I could not open it.

'The door won't open, Mr Biggs.' I felt afraid, conscious now that it really was late.

He turned the iron ring beneath the lock, and pulled backwards strongly, then placed his shoulder to the dark wood and heaved outward. But it would not open. Speechless I waited, praying desperately that it would move. The thought that Harriet might have come silently back and locked the door, gathered strength in my mind.

'It's locked,' I cried, 'I know it's locked.'

I clung to him with fear, holding his hand to my cheek, trying to ease the terror that stormed in me. It seemed as if the whole summer had been lived between the two extremes of joy and fear, and both were unbearable. I was not angry with Harriet, for I might some time, for some explicable reason, act in the same way. But I was angry, within my fear, at the circumstances that turned such simple natural things – like doors locking or time passing – into events of magnitude and worry. I could not imagine what peace the Tsar must feel at not always having to think of the hour or the place, of being answerable only to himself. I forgot until he spoke, that Mrs Biggs for him took the place of my mother.

'She'll give me half an hour more,' he said, 'assuming that it's ten o'clock. Then she'll come down the lane in search of me.'

'What about the windows?' I said carefully, unable to see his expression, but knowing that it must be weak and despairing. At least my fear was real, I had cause to be afraid; at thirteen it was natural my parents should be angry and upset if I returned late home. I was not a grown man, married thirty years, who had taken the initiative under the beech leaves. I felt elated and superior to him grown so flabby in his relationship with Mrs Biggs, and wondered if this were part of Harriet's plan.

'They're too high,' said the Tsar, looking up into the darkness. 'Besides, they only open at the top.' He moved his hands along the wall beside the door, his nails making a tiny scratching sound as they grated against the stone.

'The light switches are all outside in the porch,' I said, sounding almost gleeful in the darkness.

It was a very good plan of Harriet's, and I was sure now it was a plan.

Only she could have thought of something so exquisitely subtle, so calculated to show the Tsar as a frail creature, limited by relationships such as we knew. I had only to tell the truth at home, and most of the anger would be mitigated. 'Someone locked me in the church,' I would say, or 'A ghost shut the door. I was terrified.'

The Tsar was gliding down the church, striking matches every yard, to enable him to see better. I followed him, feeling my way with hands on the pew rows, stamping my feet down firmly so that he would know I was following. He opened a door and light flooded out across the altar steps, from the vestry. A row of white cassocks hung on pegs, frilled out and lay back again on the cream wall.

'Good,' said the Tsar, moving round the room hopefully looking for keys, face wrinkled under the bulb of electricity. We crossed eagerly from corner to corner, buoyed up with expectancy, pulling aside the cassocks and the verger's black gown, searching for keys, enjoying throwing the garments untidily to the floor. The one cupboard was bare save for an old hat of the Canon's, and a pair of small football boots. The desk under the window contained only some sticky-backed pictures issued to the Sunday school, and one woollen glove knitted in green. Everything reminscent of white-clouded Sunday afternoons – the picture on the wall that used to be in the Children's corner, the special plate for us to put our pennies in – conspired to make the night more strange, and fringed it with a lunatic delight, the delight of searching the Canon's vestry without stealth. How lovely, in spite of the lateness of the hour and the trouble no doubt to come, the situation was.

'Damn,' said the Tsar worriedly, standing in the middle of the room. There were no keys to find.

I tried to think what Harriet would do in such an extremity. Break the stained-glass windows or burn down the door with the Tsar's futile little matches? Both measures seemed equally awe-inspiring in their finality.

'Mr Biggs,' I said politely, 'we could break one of the windows.'

The Tsar was too worried to reply; he stood like a man might who had been hunted for days, and was now trapped with his back to the wall. I thought that any tender shoot of love that was to have flourished between us, was now cruelly underfoot. He must be tired and bitter at all the trouble Harriet and I had caused him. I didn't think Harriet had meant that to happen.

The Tsar leaned against the cream wall and studied the windowless room. The vestry door, though smaller than the main door into the churchyard, was as thick and sturdy, and he could never hope to force it open. He looked up at the vaulted ceiling and shook his head hopelessly.

'I'm sorry, child, God knows what time it is.'

I allowed my face to become tragic and upset.

'Don't worry.' He patted my arm bravely. 'We'll get out somehow.'

I did not feel I could convincingly remain the helpless little girl, at least not for very long. If it were left to him we might possibly die here and be found helpless and skeleton-ribbed on the vestry floor when the Canon eventually opened the church next Sunday. I said, 'Mr Biggs, I'm going to break one of the windows if I can.'

'No,' he said petulantly, 'no, be sensible. You can't do that.'

With noble face and eagle heart, remembering Mrs Biggs had called him weak, I said in my determined voice, walking to the open door, 'You'd better help me for I mean to do it.'

The church was huge and black with darkness; I had to tell myself that trees in winter looked different from those in summer, that it was only a seasonal difference. The church by day was the same as now, I had nothing to fear.

I spread my hands in front of me, coaxing the wall to come nearer, feet splayed out cautiously like a matador. In the corner near the side altar the Canon kept a window pole. I had only to feel along the brass rail and remember him Sunday upon Sunday advancing to the corner, luscious mouth parted a little, hand outstretched, and I would find it. 'God's pure air, children,' he had said as he opened the window. Triumphantly I shouted. 'It's here, Mr Biggs, come and help me.'

His voice in the darkness was low and upset. I felt sorry for him then.

'What do you want me to do?'

How often had Harriet made me feel dominated and ineffectual, so that I answered her repeated orders in just such a voice of self pity and suffering.

'Here is the window pole' – I spoke briskly to cover the giggle in my voice – 'we must put the hook in the window ring and haul ourselves up on to the sill. There's only one window we can break, the third one. You can tell it by feel. It's the only one that got damaged in the war and they replaced it with coloured glass. We have to stand against the pane and smash hard at the bottom and when it gives jump on to the grass. We both run to the gate into the woods, so that if anyone hears us we'll have plenty of cover under the trees. You run up the dunes above the tadpole ponds and I'll go over the fields near the barracks. We will be much safer if we separate.' I felt Harriet would be proud of me.

The Tsar said 'Yes' in an expressionless way, and struck a match, holding it between cupped hands till it burned more fiercely, and held it out. His eyes in the small glow of light were arched wide as he looked at length of pole I held. The expression of immense surprise faded and died as the match went out.

'Give it to me,' he said. 'You go and put off the light in the vestry.'

His hands as they circled my fingers felt dry and cold. I let go of the pole and stepped back quickly.

It took me a long time to reach the vestry, because the small light that seeped from the doorway did little to alleviate the darkness. I could look fixedly at it and make for its goal, but my feet and body moved heavily in the blackness. When I reached the door and put up my hand to the light switch I paused and thought there might be something else Harriet would wish me to do. I opened the drawer and pulled out the sticky-backed pictures and looked at them. On all of them a fair angelic Jesus stared out blindly with eyes of cobalt blue. If I had a pencil, I told myself, I would draw moustaches on them all, honestly I would. I was glad I had no pencil. I switched the light off and closed the door and stood with my back to it. I shouted, 'Where are you?'

'Here.'

I started to move cautiously back along the way I had come, moving in the direction of his voice. His breathing, agitated with effort, filled the church. 'Here,' he shouted, 'here.' When I reached him he told me to keep on striking matches to give him light to find the ring at the top of the window. Endlessly I did as he instructed. There never seemed to have been a time when we had not been imprisoned in the church among the trees. Beyond the pines the tide must have ebbed and flowed for generations without number, while we struggled to hook the pole on to the window. Then it was done. The Tsar said nothing but gave a grunt of relief. He stopped struggling and stood still, hand upstretched.

'Well done,' I said, bolstering him, although now it hardly mattered. I waited a moment before telling him what I wanted him to do because I did not like to bully.

He laughed suddenly and said, 'What an impossible position to be in,' and laughed again, this time more loudly.

'When you're ready you'd better climb on to the pew behind you and jump against the wall, both feet out to meet it. Put your hands as high up the pole as you can, so that it won't unhook as you jump.' Bravely the Tsar scrambled upright on the back of the pew. I struck a match to help him to estimate his leap but it died almost at once. He launched himself at the wall and a groan of pain rose softly out of the church.

'What's wrong?'

There was no reply, only a sound of hurried breathing and feet slithering on the stone wall. A noise of laborious crawling, as if some strange primeval crab moved towards the window sill above my head. Then I could see the dark outline of the Tsar in a tortured mass against the glass, the pole held tight to his head.

'There's nothing to hold on to.' His voice was high-pitched and distressed. 'I can't let go of the pole.'

'It's all right. Hold the pole in your left hand and move as far along the sill as you can.' It was easy to tell him, 'There's a cord round a hook on the wall. Feel for that but don't jerk the pole.' The Tsar did not move. Angrily I shouted, 'Go on, it'll be all right.'

He must have felt abandoned and furious now as he was forced to move along the thin sloping sill, seeing confused shadows of trees swaying outside in the churchyard.

I was conscious of being very tired. The effort of moving the Tsar into position, the strain of compelling him to carry out my plan made me realise the power and drive Harriet needed to be always manipulating and coaxing me along the lines she desired.

'I've found it.'

The Tsar seemed to be spreadeagled in a starfish of arms and legs against the window. The pole jutted out like a third elongated limb. I stood on the end of the pew and felt for the end of it.

'Let go,' I ordered. 'You hang on to the hook and move further over.'

He nearly fell. His body ballooned outwards, invisible hands clawing at the glass. Then he folded inwards breathing heavily. I wanted to laugh at the fuss he was making. He was so awfully bad at this sort of thing even though he had lived for years.

'Are you all right?'

'Yes. When you jump mind you don't knock your face.' I showed my teeth in the darkness and tilted out towards the wall on raised feet and hauled on the pole, pulling myself slowly up to the sill, keeping my eyes to the window, to the faint greyness that was not light but was not total darkness.

'Mr Biggs,' I said feverishly, 'Mr Biggs, I can't get any higher.' He began to edge along the sill, one hand clutching the hook in the wall, the other groping for me.

'Can you get hold of my arm?' His voice was stronger now that he was in a position to help me.

It was very difficult; the Tsar balanced on a narrow ledge grasping a pole that might slip free of its hook, and I pulling frantically at his raincoat to lever myself upright. When finally I lay along his back, crucified against him like one of the saints in the window he leaned his cheek upon, we both stayed there helpless, unable to move. If after all Harriet had come back and unlocked the door, I would not have stirred.

'You're a heavy girl,' said the Tsar at last. I hated him. I hadn't remembered that I was stout, I had thought how fragile and childlike I must seem clinging to his superior strength. I tried to ease away from him and nearly fell, clutching at him convulsively so that he groaned.

'I'm sorry. I nearly lost my balance.' He did not reply, he did not seem to breathe.

At last he asked me, 'What am I supposed to do?' He meant

more possibly than the words conveyed. A question of the future and what it was Harriet and I expected of him.

'Mr Biggs, is the pole very heavy?'

'It's an awkward length, that's all. It's too damn short to rest on the floor and too long to hold easily.'

'Well, swing it inwards and lean on the glass. If it doesn't break, let go of the pole at once.'

Secretly I doubted if the glass would even crack, so thick and hard it felt. I waited a long time, then the Tsar said, 'I'm going to try now. Are you ready?'

'Yes,' I said bravely, voice thin in the darkness.

There was a sound like ice breaking, a sharp clean noise, and then a slithering free as the pane fell out. I heard the pole fall behind me as the night air rushed to meet my face and I landed heavily on the grass. The soil was so cool and the ground so firm that I wanted just to lie there, but I stood up and ran along the path to the gate into the woods. The gate was difficult to open, jammed tight by the heap of dead flowers and wreaths that littered the path. Harriet had a collection of memoriam cards edged with black that she had salvaged from the pile. She kept them in a special folder and wrote little postscripts to each one.

'Mr Biggs!' I shouted. 'Mr Biggs!'

Such an escape we had made, how cleverly I had freed us. The trees distilled a sweet smell of beech and pine; the fragrance of summer days cradled the woods and rose up from the cinnamon brown earth. The thought that I had achieved so much without Harriet to guide me filled me with exhilaration. What mattered if I was only thirteen and my parents liked me in bed by ten o'clock. I did not care if they called the police and locked me finally in my room. The round dark wound in the side of the church, the window splattered among the graves could easily be remedied by the Tsar sending some money, without his name, to the Canon.

I was hurrying across the field that lay in front of the army camp, making for the station. When I climbed the wall into the road I saw the figure of a man crouched under the lamp at the foot of the hill. He was holding a handkerchief to his face.

'What is it, did you cut yourself?'

He looked so pale and hurt, thick blood running into his mouth. 'I banged my nose as I fell,' he said with difficulty, dabbing at his nostrils with the stained cloth. What a petty injury to have. He had smashed a window, leaped into the grass but he had only managed to bang his nose.

'How did you do that? I landed on my feet on the grass.'

'You were lucky. There's a concrete verge right round the walls.'

'Look, I must go. My parents probably have the police looking for me.'

I ran on up the hill strongly, leaving him huddled under the lamp. A car breasted the hill, fierce headlights swept my face as it slowed to the kerb.

'Dad, I'm so glad.'

I opened the door and fell inside and started to cry. 'It's been dreadful, I've been so frightened.' He was quite silent, slumped over the wheel in massive reproach.

'I was in the woods and I saw a woman running through the trees, wearing a cloak. She had blood all over her face.'

He started the engine and turned the car, driving back over the hill.

'Just before I saw her I heard a crash from the church, like a window breaking . . . it was dreadful, Dad.'

I let myself sink into the waves of grief that tore over me, spurred on by his silence, convinced he knew I was lying. We stopped outside the house and he helped me out, still not speaking. A light shone in the hall; the door was open and Mother stood on the step, small and defenceless.

'What is it, George? Is she all right?'

'God knows what the hell happened. It's beyond me.'

I was led into the kitchen. The light was so harsh I had to shut my eyes against it.

'Mother, I couldn't help it, I couldn't, it was the lady in the woods.' I clung to her unable to bear her credulous face.

'She shouldn't go into those damn woods with all those blighters from the camp roaming the blasted place.'

Throughout my story Dad's face seemed about to smile. I felt the absurdity of the story irritated him though he could not prove I was lying. My mother asked me questions sharply and coldly, but when I broke down she folded me in her arms and rocked me, big as I was, on her knee.

At last I was able to go to bed. I lay in the dark wide-eyed. I had avoided real displeasure, I had been kissed, I had explained the broken window. They would never trace it to me, the more so as Harriet had been home early. I had lied very well and cried effortlessly; I would look white and ill in the morning. I thought of the beautiful night and my god-like strength in the church and I began to smile when I remembered the Tsar's banged nose under the lamp. Harriet could not have managed better.

11

HARRIET's father saw the Tsar in the city with his arm in
a sling. Harriet said perhaps he had only sprained it when
he jumped from the window, and it was probably not a serious
injury. She offered to call on Mrs Biggs but I said it was un-
wise to go so soon after the adventure in the garden.

We talked at length about the evening I had been locked
in the church with the Tsar, but she did not say she had closed
the door. We wrote in the diary that we had been mysteriously
imprisoned by persons unknown, but I knew it was Harriet.
I wanted to ask her if it was part of the plan but I was afraid
she might call me stupid. She told me her father had said the
Tsar usually crossed the river on the ferry boat on a Wednes-
day to visit the firm's other factory.

'We'll go tomorrow,' she said. 'We'll tell them we're going
to the museum and they'll be delighted.'

'He mightn't go after all, not if his arm is bad.'

'We'll go anyway.'

We travelled on a morning train. I was made to wear my
school uniform but Harriet said it slimmed me down anyway.
We went on a tram to the docks, bouncing up and down on
the wooden seats. The landing stage was littered with papers
and refuse and old men in white mufflers sat on benches and
stared out to sea. We sat beside them for a time waiting for
the boat to come in, trying to adopt just such an attitude of
forgetfulness and isolation, but we were too alive. They did
not look directly at anything, not even at the gulls that circled
and screamed above the oily stretch of water. Harriet said

they had the view imprinted on their eyes long ago, and only thought of distant things connected with the landscape.

An old man on a bench further along began to whistle between his teeth, tapping his stick on the ground. When the red-red-robin goes bob-bob-bobbing a-long . . . A row of thin knees jerked up and down, a row of polished boots clumped in time to the tune. Any moment now, I thought, Harriet would fling arms wide and sing the words at the top of her voice. She was probably only waiting for a tired chorus of old women in shawls and tattered skirts to dance over the stones, massive bosoms a-bobbing, before she began. Seagulls flashed white wings in the sun, flying across the tin roof of the pier. The hands of the clocks that indicated the time of arrival of boats from Birkenhead and Wallasey moved jerkily into place. A woman with a pink face and yellow cardigan leaned against the rail. 'Red-red-robin,' sang Harriet loudly, stamping both feet and leaning out over the bench to smile at the row of old men. The whistling stopped, knees stiffened, boots rested heavily on the stones; the row of small eyes stared unresisting into the sun.

We sat there for two hours, waiting for the Tsar, watching each passenger patiently and carefully. I was not quite sure what we were to do or say if we did see him, and when I asked Harriet, she said, 'It doesn't really matter. The important thing is that he should see us all the time, not only on the shore or in the woods. I want him to feel hemmed in.'

I wondered if he had to feel hemmed in because he had called her evil. The love affair of the Tsar and me seemed to be forgotten. She had not even remembered to ask me if I had come to a more definite arrangement with him. She had not even asked me with great eagerness what he had said to me in the church.

When we did see the Tsar, he was with a dark handsome little man with a black moustache. They alighted from the Wallasey boat talking quickly, placing tentative hands on the rail of the gangway, the Tsar turning sideways to look at the man's face.

'Hallo, Mr Biggs,' said Harriet, screwing her face up fiendishly, standing before him with legs wide apart and hands behind her back. 'Fancy seeing you here.'

The Tsar raised his hat to her uncertainly, and Harriet said, 'We were just looking at the boats you know. We didn't know you would be here. What have you been doing?'

She smiled openly and with immense innocence at the dark little man beside the Tsar. He, like so many others, wanted immediately to confide in her. He leaned forward with a smile that was meant to be dashing, and said, 'I don't think I've had the pleasure.'

The Tsar hesitated; he seemed to shrink in the sunlight at the man's awful vulgarity.

'Two young friends of mine from Formby,' he said. 'This is Mr Douglas Hind.'

Harriet and Mr Hind embarked on one of her long ceremonial conversations.

'And what do you do with yourself these long summer days, dear?'

'Isn't that rather impertinent?'

'Oh come now . . .' the moustached man laughed delightedly.

'Harriet's father said you had your arm in a sling, Mr Biggs.'

The Tsar rubbed his wrist at the thought.

'Yes, I did, child. A bit of a sprain I think, nothing serious.'

'Was she in the road when you got home?'

He seemed to be searching the crowds on the landing stage for a familiar face. He half turned and touched his jaw with his fingers.

'No, she wasn't,' he said abstractedly.

Mr Hind laughed again, little moustache moving like a cork on the ocean of his lip.

'How did you explain your wrist?' I asked, wanting him to look at me.

'I said a boy ran into me on his bicycle,' said the Tsar.

He did not smile. He looked unhappy. I wanted to make

him happy again if Harriet would let me. Mr Hind touched the Tsar's arm. 'Peter, this young lady suggests a cup of coffee. Good idea, eh?'

He smiled frankly at the Tsar and then at Harriet.

'Yes, of course.'

The Tsar seemed to think anything would be preferable to standing in the open like this where anyone might see. Harriet and Mr Hind led the way into the snack-bar. It was all wrong, I knew that. We ought never to have spoken to him away from the shore. The trees and the church and the lane to the sea were the right borders for our relationship. It was a mistake to think we could function outside these boundaries.

The Tsar stirred his coffee and looked out of the window, stretching his neck like a boy whose pride had been hurt. He swallowed repeatedly, his Adam's apple moving unbeautifully in the thin discoloured throat.

Flies circled lightly above a plate of iced cakes on the next table; a workman in overalls and peaked cap yawned vastly, showing white gums, and blew cigarette smoke at the flies.

'Actually,' said Harriet in a sweet childish voice, 'I shall be fourteen in a few months' time. Mummy says I can cut my hair then.'

'Aaah . . . no.' Mr Hind was unbearably shaken. He stretched forth a swarthy hand and lightly touched the plait that lay on Harriet's shoulder.

'No,' he said sadly and foolishly, 'don't have it cut off.'

The Tsar gave him a swift guilty look and turned away to the window not trusting himself to speak.

'I don't think,' said Harriet, looking sorrowfully at Mr Hind, 'that Mr Biggs cares for me very much.'

Mr Hind leaned back in his chair and placed his hands behind his head, elbows spread upward like a kite.

'Surely not. You're a lucky fellow, Peter.'

He dipped his body and dug at the Tsar's shoulder with one sharp elbow.

'I believe I am.' The Tsar relaxed, sprawling a little over the table, eyes of friendship twinkling at Mr Hind.

They were friends and confidants, I was sure. Even friends such as Harriet and I were, but separated by different ways of life. The Tsar had probably told him about the night in the church, but vulgarly, to match the mood of the moustached man. He had said, 'Locked in – imagine, Douglas. Had me scampering over a window ledge with a damn big window pole.' 'What happened before that, eh?' Mr Hind had asked with sly insinuation. 'Oh, I tried to kiss the girl, but she wasn't having any.' Then they had both laughed loudly.

Fascinated I watched the charred moustache springing above the moist mouth. The Tsar was so frail and yellow-skinned beside this man. He seemed to be made of hair. It waved crisply over his round head, growing down to the tips of his ears. Eyebrows, lashes, cheek-bones, lip, all dark and quivering with black hair. Hands, throat and neck shadowed with its profusion, Mr Hind spun and glowed in the sunlight. Under the table two legs brown and hard were covered too with a pelt of fur. It was as if a bumble bee hovered with three moths and the Tsar was the palest of the three.

Harriet kicked my ankle with her shoe. I supposed Mr Hind was pressing her knee under the table, so I looked at her with a sympathetic excitement that conveyed something of envy too, and she glowed at me across the table, mouth curved at the corner in a pleased small smile of satisfaction. My envy was real because no one ever pressed my knee so quickly or so daringly, and though it was quite likely that Harriet had pressed his knee first I could not be so definite with the Tsar. I comforted myself with the thought that I was the more feminine and refined. The Tsar said, 'Were your parents very worried about you the other night?'

I might truthfully have replied that they were very worried but it was always more romantic to be the neglected child.

'No, they were out drinking with friends. They never seem to notice whether I'm there or not.'

In another situation I would have said my parents had cried and phoned the police in their worry, and even that would have sounded a lie, so long ago had Harriet and I forgotten how to tell the truth. The clock on the wall of the building opposite chimed the hour. The Tsar consulted his watch for accuracy and put his hand on the edge of the table in preparation to rise.

'Tsar.' I had to speak very quietly in case Harriet overheard. 'Tsar, will you be going to the woods tonight?'

He looked at me startled, the hand braced against the table edge relaxed slowly, his body leaned forward once more over the coffee cups. Quick, quick, I thought, before Harriet stops talking, say something, Mr Biggs. His eyes narrowed suddenly as I watched him, his expression was almost of distaste. I blinked rapidly and moved my lips to change my own expression. How often had Harriet recoiled from me, telling me I was ugly, that I must modify and govern the muscles of my face. It was not that my feelings illuminated and transformed me, as Harriet became transformed in diabolical anger or joy, it was more a dreadful eagerness and vulnerability that made my face like an open wound, with all the nerves exposed and raw.

Weakly the Tsar said, 'I expect so . . .' The little boy swallowed nervously, blinking back the tears of self-pity, red eyelids fluttering.

'Not in the road though. Behind the church.'

He spoke very quickly, as if Mrs Biggs might be within earshot. The hand pushed against the table, this time with decision, and he rose to his feet. Mr Hind regretfully removed his hand from Harriet's leg and stood beside him.

When they had gone Harriet sat well back in her chair and smiled warmly at me. I wanted to tell her at once about my arrangement with the Tsar, but I knew she wanted to be quiet. The man in overalls pushed his plate away noisily and stretched himself, lifting his cap for a moment to ease his hot forehead. Harriet said, 'Mrs Biggs is going away next week for two days, and Mr Hind is coming to keep the Tsar company.'

'Oh.'

How clever Harriet was to find out something so important from a stranger. All the satisfaction I had felt at my mumbled request to the Tsar dissolved away, and left me humble.

'How clever you are, Harriet. How did you ask him?'

'I didn't.' She looked at me in surprise. 'He told me himself. I just led the conversation along certain lines and he told me all I wanted to know. Mrs Biggs leaves early Tuesday morning and Mr Hind and the Tsar will be alone till Thursday.'

'Oh.'

'Mr Hind suggested we might call round Tuesday evening and drink coffee.'

Even Harriet was impressed by this. Drinking coffee was part of a way of life alien to us; it went with concert and theatre going, and people who played bridge of an evening. Seeing a man on the train in the summer, wearing a neat little suit of small check and shoes of honey-coloured suede, one could say with contempt that he drank coffee after his meal. But oh the stylish little panel in the back of his jacket, that flared out like a skirt frill as he alighted on the platform. Anyone who called in the evening to the homes we knew wore gun-metal trousers and green jackets, and at nine o'clock they were given tea and fancy cakes. They were always invited, never unexpected. People who arrived unheralded were rare indeed and Harriet's mother, had such an occasion arisen, would have talked about it for days with a mixture of pride and bravado. 'No,' she would say, 'we didn't expect them, they just dropped in. Strange, wasn't it?' And a small baffled smile of pleasure would gently curve her mouth.

We both sat silent, imagining the scene at the house of the Tsar, drinking coffee out of thin white cups, locked together in the lamplight with the two men: the delicious secrecy of the night, the unfamiliar bitter taste of the dark liquid, the fearful danger, footsteps coming up the path, the Tsar crumpling paper-pale against the window as Mrs Biggs returned before time and fitted her key in the locked door. It was a lovely fearful thing to imagine, and we kept the image of it all the way to the station.

On the train I told Harriet casually that I had asked the Tsar to meet me in the woods behind the church, but she said nothing, merely nodding her head and staring out at the flying hedges and fields.

In the evening I almost hoped my mother would tell me I ought to stay indoors, but when I put my coat on in the back kitchen she smiled and told me merely to be in before it grew dark. So I had to go out. I felt excited as I turned the bend of the road and saw the church, remembering the broken window and the helplessness of the Tsar. I climbed the low wall demurely in case he was watching me, and stood among the cold ivy with thoughtful face. Everything seemed damp and sallow, the horizon was flushed green, so that there was no longer a division between earth and sky. The whole world looked sickly and weak; tombstones, slate church and pebbled path tinged with a green unhealthy light. It was as if the churchyard had been modelled with wax and placed under an enormous dome of glass, causing tiny particles of moisture to ooze and dribble along its inner surface. I could not move, so heavy had my limbs become; if I raised my foot only a little it might grow slack and slide away from me. All the time I kept the thoughtful sad look on my face in case the Tsar should see me. A small wind bustled along the pines and crept over the grass. The leaves of ivy trembled against my legs and my hair swayed and hung over my face, freeing me. I walked over the grass and the Tsar and the Canon came out suddenly and stood in the porch talking together. The Canon moved an arm up and down constantly, like a broken wing on a black crow, and the Tsar stared out into the graveyard and nodded his head. I was quite near them if I measured nearness by the relation of my body to the porch, but they looked tiny and distant, creatures under a microscope. The Canon's bulk seemed curiously whittled down and the Tsar stood a motionless yellow doll, with limp head and face of wax. I must not imagine things, I told myself. I must not imagine things. Even if my nose and ears seemed filled with cottonwool and I was moving in and out, out and in like a child's fist, I must not imagine things. A foolish smile formed on my face for the benefit of the two men.

'Why should anyone do that, Mr Biggs, do you think? Such a big expensive pane of glass.'

The Canon's voice seemed full of tears. He lisped his vowels firmly and loudly and pointed with showmanship at the piece of hardboard that had been wedged into the aperture, a blind eye among healthy ones. The Tsar hung his head and swung his hat between his fingers.

'Who did it?' I asked bravely, gazing at the Canon's petulant face and the brown eyes so filled with love. It was his eyes first and then his voice that Harriet said made you know he was senile. He shook his head ponderously from side to side, admitting, 'We do not know, we do not know.'

I could not bear the gaze of those luminous eyes, the tiny flecks of yellow light that pitted the brownness. I looked down at my feet in embarrassment and saw against my shoe a piece of glass stained dull red.

'May I keep it?'

'Of course.'

A mandarin smile narrowed his eyes, and a network of wrinkles spread out joyously across his face as the heavy mouth thinned to a line of pure sweetness. It was a terrible smile. Harriet had said he was like the witch in Hansel and Gretel who had a house made of sweets and candy, only instead of a house it was he himself who was made of sugar.

'If we broke a piece off him,' she said, 'even a bit of his little finger, it would be sweet through and through.'

And now when he smiled I felt against my tongue a fearful cloying stickiness, as if I had bitten his fingers.

'Thank you.'

I stood there uncertainly, holding the fragment of glass in my palm. The Canon wished me good night with beautiful courtesy and the Tsar smiled gravely as he was led away. I watched them go through the gap in the fence into the Canon's garden and along the path to the vicarage. The Tsar did not even signal with his hand behind the Canon's back, he just swayed delicately towards the house and turned the corner, leaving me in the porch.

He would make extravagant gestures with his hands, bring the quick tears to his eyes, and not once remember me. But I wanted him to talk to me tonight, I wanted to wait breathlessly and painfully for him to kiss me, I wanted to tell Harriet how powerfully I had questioned him. I willed him with all my strength to come back, but moments passed and I was plump and foolish in the darkening porch. Appalled, I walked round to the other side of the church and sat with my back to the fence, hunching up my knees about my face. Each time I looked up and thought, Now surely he must come, the yard was deserted. Once I heard a rustling in the woods behind me and looked half fearfully over my shoulder expecting him, but all was still, 'Keine mensch, my love,' I whispered deeply into my folded arms and smiled knowingly to myself. I felt such an ache, as if I was yawning deep inside my chest, and when the tears came I sat astonished because I did not feel unhappy. I'm just emotional, I told myself between sobs, and buried my face in my arms. If he came now he would grow pale and very gentle with me, he would . . . but I did not know what he would do. Then I remembered Mrs Biggs on the couch and the darkened room, the death's head against the leather back, and I shut my eyes so tight that the tears stopped abruptly.

'I'm going home,' I said loudly, 'I'm going home.'

I had to sit a long while in the field at the bottom of the hill for my face to become less swollen. And I really had not felt so very unhappy.

12

Harriet arranged that we should go separately to Timothy Street. She was to walk an elaborate detour round the village and approach the house over the fields. I was to come by the usual route and meet her at the house of the Tsar. On no account were we to enter the door together; singly we might go unrecognised and if one of us was caught then the other would be safe. Harriet was to arrive ten minutes ahead of me and leave the high gate open. If the gate was shut I was to walk past and walk straight home. 'Don't turn round,' she warned me as if afraid Mrs Biggs would turn me into a pillar of salt. 'I promise,' I said.

'And don't you dare say your mother wouldn't let you out. If you don't turn up I won't speak to you ever.'

My mother was busy making a dress for Frances when I left. I kissed her cheek, avoiding the row of pins caught between her lips. The high gate was open but I walked on, turning back at the end of the road and approaching it as a runner might a difficult hurdle, very fast and not looking to right or left. I rang the bell firmly, patted my hair smooth, rubbed my hand roughly across my mouth to make it red, performing these actions with feverish haste so as not to be caught when the door opened.

It was Harriet who let me in, face flushed, her plaits loose and the colourless hair hanging about her ears.

'Yes, it's her,' she called into the house and whispered quickly to me, 'don't refuse a drink but sip it slowly.' Harriet shut the front door behind us. I stood there wondering why she thought I might refuse the coffee and why I should only sip it. Perhaps there was not enough to go round. There was a grandfather clock in an alcove; it shivered and jangled its brass weights as we trod past.

It was not the dreaded front-room, it was a smaller one at the rear of the house overlooking the garden and the fields beyond. The relief at not having to sit on the blue leather couch was overwhelming. Mr Hind sat on the arm of a chair, swinging his muscular leg; the Tsar stood with shrivelled face, smiling shakily.

'Well, well, come on in, dear,' he said loudly.

Mr Hind continued to balance on the arm of the chair, watching his brown shoe as it rose and fell. He wore a blue striped suit and a waistcoat of brown felt with a watch chain across it. They were awfully like our fathers, both of them.

'Well, well,' echoed Harriet, placing her hands childishly behind her back, staring unblinkingly at the Tsar.

They were both very nervous; we had thrived and matured on such situations and had the advantage.

'Oh Harriet,' I cried, 'look, a piano!'

I sat down, perched on a velvet-topped stool, placing my hands on the keys. The only tune I knew was 'The Fairy Wedding Waltz' and I played one bar.

'Do go on,' said Mr Hind.

'I couldn't possibly,' I said truthfully. 'I'm not a bit musical.'

Harriet laughed, an easy relaxed sound of amusement, and Mr Hind coughed.

The Tsar poured a drink out of a decanter and came across the room to me, holding his glass like a flower. He sat on the stool beside me and swirled the mixture in the bowl of the glass, looking over his shoulder at Harriet and Mr Hind. I folded my hands together and stared down at the keyboard. The Tsar leaned his elbow carefully on the notes, so carefully there was no sound at all, and crossed his legs. I had only to turn sideways a little and we would face each other. Instead I sat apparently lost in thought, slack hands cupped in my lap.

'Do you think you ought not to have come?' he asked

quietly, shading his eyes with his hand, arching his palm about his brow as if to shut out a too bright light.

'Oh no, it's just, it's just . . .'

'Well, what?' He paused kindly, anxious to help me. Try as I might I could not be sincere, I could not begin to be truthful.

'It seems wrong to be here in your house, when she is away. She would suffer so if she knew.'

The skin puckered round his shadowed eyes. He massaged his forehead, kneading it unhappily, mouth drawn down in misery.

'She won't know, God willing.'

God willing was like when my father at Christmas picked up his glass of port and raised it high, saying good-humouredly, 'To absent and sea-faring friends!' There were no absent and sea-faring friends, just as the Tsar knew there was no God willing to keep our visit from Mrs Biggs. Still, it had to be said, to preserve the formalities.

'Why have you come?'

The question was so sudden and so unlike him that for a moment I was almost shocked into telling the truth.

'I wanted to see what it would be like. I mean I only know you on the shore and in the lane. It's . . . it's interesting to see where people live.'

The mouth twitched uncontrollably. The word 'interesting' had hurt him.

'I see.'

He did not see, but it was again a game and the rule was not to enlighten him; Harriet would appreciate that later when I retold the conversation. I did not want him to be hurt, though.

'I mean I like seeing you and I wanted to know how you looked inside a house.'

Mr Hind rose to his feet energetically and went to the table and its decanter. Harriet said gaily, 'Only a very little one, honest.'

The word 'honest', recalling school, seemed out of place in the room. I imagined her arm lifted in mock reproach, her

bright eyes smiling at Mr Hind. The Tsar looked at her between his fingers and away again, and now I knew her arm had
dropped into her lap, and the bold eyes no longer laughing
were staring at him curiously. Mr Hind stood in front of the
Tsar.

'You haven't offered the young lady a drink yet.'

He shook a finger roguishly at the man on the stool and
asked me, 'What will it be, my dear? Sherry or a little whisky?'

Such a confiding smile, the moist mouth very red and lively
beneath the thick moustache.

'Whisky, I think.'

I turned on the stool, away from the Tsar and towards
Harriet, but she sipped at her drink demurely and would not
look up.

'Right you are.'

Mr Hind turned his muscular back to me and stooped over
the decanter. The Tsar sat heavily and in silence, one hand
almost obscuring his face. The blurred edge of his jaw and the
fold of skin above his collar seemed to express reproach.

'Is whisky all right?' I asked, sounding timid.

'Whisky's very much all right.' Mr Hind stood on the
carpet, swaying from the waist, offering me the small glass
half-filled with brown liquid. I had a confused image of him
sharing a room at night with the Tsar, unbuttoning his city
shirt to expose his virile chest, and the Tsar turning his back
to thrust withered white arms into his pyjama jacket.

Mr Hind returned to Harriet.

I sipped experimentally at the drink I held, and shuddered
at the bitter taste. I had tasted it before, when I had been ill
in bed with a chill, and once when I had a period pain. It did
not seem possible that one drank it for enjoyment.

'It's very warm once it's inside,' I told the Tsar.

'Do your parents go out drinking a lot?' He looked down
at his glass.

'Not all that often. It's a relaxation.'

'Just as well they do, eh?' He gave me a gentle smile and
rubbed at his cheek. 'You wouldn't be allowed out so often.'

'They don't bother about me. I've always run wild, that's why I was sent away to school.' I felt very wronged suddenly. 'They don't understand me.'

I realised at once I had said a silly thing; it was such an obvious remark. Why, if the Tsar understood the game he had even been waiting for me to say it.

The Tsar gazed at Harriet and Mr Hind in the far corner under the window, the light fading now in the garden outside, and said:

'When you are young you think the tragedy of life is not being understood – not having the chances or the right books to read. When you are a few years wiser you know that nothing is so sad as the injustices of old age.'

'But you're not old, Tsar, not nearly old.'

I knew what he meant. I knew that my saying he was not old would make him sure I had misunderstood, but perversely I did not care.

'Why, you're quite young you know.'

'I was twenty-six when I married.' His eyes grew red-rimmed as if he was about to cry. 'I did not want to marry, I just drifted into it. I don't really regret it.' He sounded surprised, his eyes opened wider.

I fidgeted on the stool, rubbing my hands along the soft velvet, enjoying the soft touch of my frizzed hair as it fell against my cheeks when I hung my head. I could not possibly this evening make him say he loved me, even if Harriet and Mr Hind left us alone. He was not in the mood; he was all sorrow for himself and surprise that he did not regret marrying Mrs Biggs. He oozed astonishment and self-pity; a kind word would stretch him sobbing across the piano in a wild welter of discordant notes. Mrs Biggs had said he was weak, that a little more self control would help. Doubtless she was right; she might be the one who was the more sinned against.

'Why did you marry if you did not really want to marry?'

There was no answer. Helplessly I felt Harriet's eyes on my back, ears strained to catch the conversation. I forgot she had told me to sip at the drink; I shut my eyes and swallowed quickly, and placed the empty glass on the piano top.

The room was very warm, I was aware of a wetness on my palms. Harriet began to laugh. It was her exhibitionist laugh and very realistic. I looked over my shoulder and saw Mr Hind with his hand on her hair, and Harriet, half hidden by him and the breadth of his shoulders, leaning back in the chair with her head right back and her mouth wide open. Mr Hind any moment was meant to kiss the open mouth to stop her laughing, and even as I watched his head bent suddenly and Harriet became quiet. I turned away and looked at my miserable Tsar.

The Tsar uncovered his eyes and glanced quickly at the empty glass. He frowned at it.

'I forgot I had to sip at it,' I said. 'Will I be drunk now?'

'You know how we got this house?' He sounded angry with me, as if I had prompted the question. I wondered if he were drunk, and if he was would it be easier to make him kiss me.

'No, how?'

'She won it in a raffle. Yes, she did; that's how we got it.'

'Really.' For all the world I sounded like Harriet's mother indulging in a slightly risky conversation and handling it in a ladylike way.

'Someone had a bazaar down at the church . . . before the Canon's time. They had tickets for this house, and she bought one. That's why we got married, because she won the raffle. Seemed the only sensible thing to do.'

'Yes, but . . .' Supposing they had won a ship, not a house, would he have gone to sea? Or a horse . . . he might have been a jockey.

'You could have sold the house.'

'Oh no, you had to live in it or forfeit it. You had to play fair.' He was quite right, I could see that now. You had to play fair.

Mr Hind and Harriet were opening the door. I sat motionless on the piano stool, unable to call for help. 'Harriet,' I might have said loudly, 'Harriet, it's getting out of hand. He's crying.' But the door shut and we were alone.

The Tsar appeared not to notice. He stood up and went to the decanter to fill his glass.

'It's funny you know, how things happen . . .' He swung round to stare at me, one hand holding the decanter by the neck. 'Just a little ticket . . . a little ticket and you get married and settle down.'

The whisky poured steadily into his glass; he stood, one leg bent at the knee, his eyes watching, his hand pouring. I hoped he would not realise how like a bad poem he sounded. Harriet would say it was because most people had unoriginal minds, but I could not think just then how else he could paraphrase his existence.

Darkness settled along the neglected garden; leaves rustled frantically in a sudden small wind.

'What number was the ticket?'

Something so important must remain for ever engraved upon the memory.

'The number?' He became irritated. 'Lord, how would I know. Thirteen most likely.'

He sat down beside me on the piano stool. His elbow this time struck with elation on the notes, making ugly musical sounds. 'All I know is, she won the raffle.'

If he was not drunk he was being very clever. Perhaps he thought it would be easier to kiss me if I thought he was drunk. I wondered what Harriet was doing to Mr Hind. Now was the time to start saying the Lord's Prayer; I had waited long enough. If he did not kiss me before Thine is the Kingdom, he would not kiss me tonight.

The Tsar crossed one thin leg over the other, and drank a little of the whisky.

Our Father which art in heaven . . .

'I go into her room now and then, once in perhaps six months. Usually it's after a night out with Douglas Hind. She never says a word.'

But what about the evening on the couch. He wasn't telling

the truth. Hallowed be Thy name, Thy Kingdom come . . .

'Other times she tries to sit on my knee . . . It's dreadful, she's too heavy. I get cramp. Wouldn't do to let her know though.'

Thy will be done, as it is in Heaven. That was wrong surely.

'Sometimes she comes into my room in a blue nightdress she had when we first got married. I lie there with my eyes shut, praying she'll go away.'

It was horrible. I could not listen to such words. Harriet must be wrong. He was far too old, far too sad to be helped or turned into an experience. He put a hand on my shoulder, and I leant sidewàys under his weight. He placed his glass carefully on the piano top, shut his eyes, and laid his forehead against my cheek.

'I should like,' he said formally, 'to kiss you, my dear.' But he just remained folded against me, almost as if he slept. Please, please, I thought, I'm sorry, I'm sorry, bring it to an end. Two tears rolled off his cheeks and down my face. He smelled like an invalid who had been too long out of the sun. He sat back blindly on the stool, took me by the shoulders as if to steady a moving target, and brought his tear-stained face closer.

Dryness on my lips, a sour smell of drink, his knee with its too sharp bone pressing into my leg; such clumsiness in his whole gesture. I felt so weary I wanted to lean back and pretend to be ill. It was terrible to be kissed by him. I closed my eyes and thought what I should say when he had finished. I must look long and wonderingly at him and say presently, 'You make me feel funny.' He did not make me feel funny, not as the Italian had when he called me a Dirty Little Angel, but I would have to say so, otherwise he would feel hurt. Besides I did not know what else to say. All the time I kept wondering why I had felt I loved him, why I had loved him on the shore and when I was with Harriet, and why I did not love him now when he kissed me. His mouth relaxed its pressure, a flat little sound of air escaped as his face drew away from mine. I had no time to look long and wonderingly at him, no time to say anything; he pushed at me fiercely so that I slipped and lay along the stool, and all the time he kept his eyes closed.

'Please don't,' I said politely. 'It's awfully uncomfortable.'

On his knees beside the stool the Tsar shuffled to hold my hands in his. He laid his head on my hip and said :

'You're so young. You're so young. I love you. I love you.'

I looked at the chair by the fireplace, and the framed picture on the wall above it, memorising positions so nothing should be lost when I told Harriet. I did not dare smile though, in case he opened his eyes.

I touched the thin skull with my hand, and stroked the hair to soothe him, remembering as I did so the evening by the tadpole ponds when I dreamed of this moment. Tears ran down his face, making him ridiculous. I could not forget my conventional upbringing, my instilled belief that it was not right for a man to cry. His hands moved, they spread out over my knee and he bent his head and cried through his fingers. I pushed at his wrists with all my strength, and he looked up quickly and stared in astonishment, a look of bewilderment in the distressed eyes, as if he could not believe I was unwilling to comfort him. Then with cunning he pressed his face against my leg and held on to me, the tears spilling on to my skin.

The room was almost dark, the house quite silent; Harriet and Mr Hind were lost somewhere in the upstairs rooms.

'Please don't,' I whispered. 'Please don't, Mr Biggs.'

Twilight flutterings, peevish struggling; fingers like goldfish squirmed and flickered to be free. Back and forth in a dim aquarium the Tsar and I threshed with our hands. He fought desperately to find a reservoir for his grief, and suddenly the strength and the will left me. I lay still and turned my face away from him because I did not want him to see my expression should he look up.

I knew I could comfort him; I could be kind and good and heal him; but I would not. I imagined his sobs must be more from shame and self-pity than from sadness, so I just sat there and stored up the experience inside me.

I looked down unsmiling at the top of his head, at the soft

skin showing beneath the crown of his hair, at the taut neck stretched over my knee. It was happening so differently from the way I had imagined, even if he had said he loved me. He had not demanded that I love him in return, that I should give myself to him. He had not told me that I was not fat but thin and golden. So I would not be kind to him, I would not lift a finger to show my sympathy. And then it was he slipped away from me and lay face downwards on the carpet at my feet. He lay so abjectly, shoulders lifting a little as he wept, that I stood up in embarrassment, not knowing what to do. I touched him gently with the toe of my shoe, and he moved convulsively and clutched at my foot with his hands. And while I stood there helplessly, the Tsar with my foot in his two hands, and his head buried in the carpet, the light was switched on, and I heard Harriet laugh. She stood in the doorway, arms folded over her chest, and laughed her exhibitionist laugh. She did not look at me, but kept her eyes fixed on the Tsar, to punish him. He had looked up into the light and stared at her in the doorway. I was glad she did not point at the door and tell me to go home and not turn round. I looked curiously at the Tsar. He lay quite still, face of grief yellow in the harsh light, small head straining upward. I did not understand why Harriet was laughing. The Tsar looked comical enough, but the plan after all was to make him fall in love with me.

After this last indignity he would never wish to see me again. Mr Hind, furry mouth apart in surprise, pulled at Harriet's arm worriedly.

'Steady on,' he said, not looking at the Tsar. He pulled more harshly at her, dragging her backwards into the dark hall, and closed the door. Slowly the Tsar bent his head and got to his knees. He got up on to his feet neatly and turned to the window, staring thoughtfully out into the garden. Harriet's voice rose loudly in anger beyond the door; Mr Hind was silent, speechless before her unaccountable rage.

Moments passed as the harsh light penetrated deeper into the room. The carpet under my feet became a lighter grey, drab flowers struggled outward in a tangled pattern across its surface; the piano, which in the darkness had filled the room, shrivelled at my back and was unimportant.

'I think,' said the Tsar, 'we had better all have some coffee.'

He stood still, arms slack against his sides, thin hands idle. Finally he coughed, a small dry sound that reassured him, and went out into the hall leaving the door open. When the light was first switched on and the Tsar exposed so foolishly, I had not dared smile. Now, alone, I did not want to smile. It did not seem very funny.

If he had scrambled at once to his feet, face comic in dismay, I would have laughed. But to lie there quite still in front of Harriet, head rearing like a tortoise, lined face so grieved and sad, had spoiled the scene. I felt I should have comforted him so that he need not have lain on the floor for Harriet to laugh at him. It was my fault and I felt guilty.

Harriet came into the room with Mr Hind. Her anger was gone; she smiled kindly at me and leaned against the mantelpiece.

'You should see upstairs,' she told me. 'Why, there's two rooms full of boxes filled with postcards and things, all scattered over the floors.'

'Two rooms . . . how wonderful. Are there really, Mr Hind?' I did not look at him and he did not reply.

'It's true, isn't it, Douglas?'

Evidently Harriet had been very harsh with Mr Hind, and was now willing to forgive him. He drooped in his armchair by the grate, face sullen. All his charm had deserted him, his moustache lay heavily and without life across his lip.

'Yes,' he said shortly.

Harriet said, 'And we found a telegram sent to Mrs Biggs on her wedding day. "Wishing you every happiness today and always, Meg and Wilfred." Didn't we, Douglas?'

'Yes,' said Mr Hind.

He seemed suddenly to be very sorry for Mrs Biggs. He crossed his legs and swung a resentful foot.

'I read the other day,' said Harriet, looking at me seriously, 'about a woman who collected elephants. She only managed twelve, but think how fortunate we are that it's only postcards for Mrs Biggs.'

She looked at Mr Hind innocently. If Mr Hind did not respond soon the evening would be a farce.

'I also read somewhere,' she continued, 'about a man who had a passion for collecting egg shells. He planted things in them.'

'What things?' I asked, feeling smothered by the laughter inside me.

'Just things,' said Harriet sternly, and added, 'mostly herbs, I gather.'

Mr Hind looked at her without understanding. He relented and laughed briefly. He thought no doubt that Harriet was an odd girl, pale with anger one moment and talking nonsense the next. Mr Hind did not matter, however; he was a shallow man and insensitive. It was the Tsar who must be amused and won over.

'I'll just see if I can help Mr Biggs with the coffee.' I walked quickly out into the hall and shut the door. The Tsar stood smoking a cigarette in the kitchen. He looked tidy, clean, and matter-of-fact. He had brushed his hair carefully and I thought he had washed his face. Pale smoke drifted across his eyes as he exhaled, so that I could not see his expression.

'I don't think Harriet meant to laugh.'

I stopped, not knowing how to make it sound convincing. 'I don't think she laughed because it was funny, Mr Biggs. It's just she gets angry sometimes.'

The Tsar took two blue cups from a shelf above my head, then another two, and found saucers for them. He arranged them neatly on a black tray painted with golden dragons, and opened a cupboard by the door.

'Don't worry about my feelings, my dear.' His back was to me as he said it, and his voice sounded cold, as if the light, that had so savagely been switched on, had in some way hardened him and drained away his weakness.

'It's you I'm concerned about. You and Harriet.'

119

He lifted down a green bowl carefully and turned and placed it on the Chinese tray.

'There . . . all ready I think.'

In the sitting-room he poured coffee and handed cups to Harriet and Mr Hind without embarrassment. I thought it strange that he was so at ease until I remembered the night Harriet and I had seen him on the couch, and all the other nights there must have been that I did not know about but could imagine. Harriet sat up straight in her chair, her eyes bright, two round dabs of colour on her pale cheeks. She did not look at the Tsar.

And he, unsmiling, talked a little to Mr Hind about business, and did not look directly at any of us.

Harriet tried to salvage something from the evening, but she sounded dispirited and I could only lean back in my chair and balance the coffee cup on my knee and feel hopeless.

When Harriet finally stood up in the small room and, raising her arms above her head in an unconscious gesture of surrender, said, 'We must go, it's very late,' Mr Hind sprang to his feet almost with relief and said he would see us to the door.

The two men were now alert once more; they were impatient for us to leave them. They had both drawn away from us and it was not only the scene of an hour earlier that had caused the withdrawal. Even if Harriet had not switched on the light and stood laughing in the doorway they would have been anxious for us to leave. The effort of appearing young and in sympathy with us was beginning to show.

The Tsar said good night to me at the door. He did not wait to see us go through the gate. The door shut and they must have turned the hall light off immediately because I stumbled a little in the darkness and jostled against Harriet.

'Be careful,' she snapped.

'You shouldn't have laughed at him like that.'

'I know. It was that stupid bugger Hind. I can't bear –'

'What was wrong with him then?'

' – men like that. Honest, when you think he's married and bringing up children it makes you despair. He's a cretin.'

'I thought you liked him.'

At the corner of the lane she said briskly, 'I'll see you to-morrow. Good night.'

Nothing more, no chat, no questions.

I began to wonder if it was deliberate, the way she no longer discussed things with me. Maybe she was letting me go. She still had to point me in the required direction but she was no longer holding my hand. I did not think I liked it.

13

I N the morning my mother asked me to go over the line for a loaf of bread. Harriet was leaning on her gate. 'Come in,' she said. 'There's a lot I want you to write in the diary. I've been thinking all night.'

Seeing the expression on my face, she added, 'It's all right. The little woman's gone to have her hair done.'

'What have you been thinking about?'

'Lots of things.'

In her room I opened the diary and she said, 'We have been to have coffee with the man and his friend, and he deliberately made himself an object of pity and ridicule. He lay weeping on the floor and did not try to hide himself. When she laughed at him to punish him he became strong and gratified. This is not good.' The words were in ink; they could not be rubbed out, unless I tore a page from the book and burnt it. I felt ashamed.

Weakly I tried to argue with her. 'It seems so cruel, Harriet. I'm sure he wasn't glad to be laughed at. We can't be sure. You've said often and often that there are dozens of reasons for people behaving in a certain way, and that one person dare not presume to know which reason is the most likely. You've said that, haven't you?' Harriet closed her eyes and leaned her head against the side of the bed. For a moment I feared she was not going to talk to me, that she was in one of her superior moods. But quite soon she opened her eyes and looked at my worried face.

'Yes,' she said, 'I have. But just sometimes I know what the real reason is. You'll just have to accept that.'

'But, Harriet, it doesn't sound right.'

I rubbed the back of my hand over the page I had written and shook my head hopelessly : 'It sounds all wrong. It's not what I felt.'

I felt warm suddenly and almost happy. Harriet and I were talking together again as we had last summer and all the summers before. She was not racing on ahead making me feel heavy and stupid. She said kindly, seriously :

'If it sounds all wrong it's because of the way it's written, not what it means. All the best parts in the book were written years ago when we didn't know the proper names for things. We are limited now by knowing how to express ourselves. It sounds worse perhaps, but we can't go back.'

'If we put "There was a piano in the room",' I said, 'and that we drank whisky, it would sound more real.'

'But the whisky and the piano wasn't real,' cried Harriet. She sat up and stared at me fiercely, her under lip thrust outward. She clenched her hands so tight the knuckles whitened.

'Don't you see – only the Tsar was real and his weeping at your feet.'

I kept silent and nodded my head. She was wrong, she must be. All very well to say the piano wasn't real when she had not lain across it. Perhaps she had not understood what I meant. I tried to think of other instances in the book, experiences we had written about that sounded real, but I couldn't.

I looked at Harriet's hands as they lay in her lap and saw thankfully they were loose and inert.

'I often think,' she said quietly, looking at her idle hands, 'that we've passed the best bit in ourselves.'

She looked at me almost pleadingly.

'I mean we'll never be as good or clever as we have been. We start going back again now.'

I wished Harriet would not tell me such things. I had such belief in her and faith, that whatever she told me I accepted utterly, and most of the things she made me believe nowadays were painful. It seemed dreadful that at thirteen I had reached my best, that I could never be any better.

'But you said it would be wonderful when we were older. You promised that we'd be full of truth with all the experiences, and see beautiful things. You promised, Harriet.'

But all the time I felt it was true. I would never be better than I had been, all my life.

Harriet began to laugh, but affectionately.

'You look so sad, as if you hadn't known it all the time. Who's going to have a pony after the war?'

I had to laugh. That was a great joke. During the war our parents had told us, 'After the war I'll buy you a pony.' The war had been over a long time now and the ponies had never been mentioned again. It was because our parents wanted to believe everything was going to be all right that they had promised such a thing. And now, whenever we yearned, half-unbelievingly, after the unattainable, we teased ourselves and used the mythical pony as a symbol of all impossible things.

'Go home,' said Harriet, closing the diary. 'Your mum will only carry on if you don't get the loaf.'

After all the rain, the little square of grass in front of the house was green; the poor sandy soil in the borders appeared healthily black and moist. It was good for roses and lupins and Sweet Williams as long as my father bought tons of manure from the farm. During the war we had grown potatoes at the back, carrots too, and he had made an air-raid shelter where now the roses climbed. Harriet said it was pathetic, a hole in the ground with a lid of tin. Like going to sea in a matchbox. There was a shelter in the back field for all the houses, but my mother said not very nice people went there, so in the end we stayed under the mahogany table in the front-room. Everyone went to the farm for manure to grow their roses in the sand. Even so if my father heard a horse going down the lane he would run out with a bucket and spade and scrape up the dung. All the gardens sprouted flowers ringed with black droppings, alive with flies. My mother in her gardening gloves hovered over the blooms, bare legs blue-veined in the calf and wasted. Sometimes she wore an old straw hat, but this afternoon the sun shone on her dry hair and burnt her neck.

I lay on the front porch, stretched out on the red-brick tiles. Frances swung on the gate and sang loudly. A small dog from the house opposite trotted over the road and sniffed at her feet. She stooped down to touch him and he leapt sideways and padded back to his side of the road, nose to the hot surface, tail quivering and agitated. He climbed the low bank into the copse of elms before the farm, and crashed noisily down into the darkness and coolness of the foxgloves and nettles. Frances sang on, stomach pressed to the top of the gate, riding the structure like a wooden horse, patting an imaginary nose as she galloped across the deserted plains.

Behind my closed eyes I relived the evening spent with the Tsar. I led up to it carefully, deliberately postponing the moment I most wanted to remember. I waited for Harriet to get up from her chair and leave the room; in slow motion I slid sideways along the piano stool and offered my mouth to the Tsar. And just as I felt I was remembering most vividly, and the feeling of warmth was just within my reach, I opened my eyes and saw my mother sitting back on her heels in the grass, wiping her hot face with a clumsy glove.

'It's so hot,' she told me, satisfied. For a moment her eyes looked coldly at me as if she read my thoughts, and in my confusion I buried my head in my arms and mumbled it was too hot.

'Why don't you read a book?' she asked me relentlessly. 'Get a deck-chair from the greenhouse and sit in the shade.'

'No, I'm all right here.'

'You're too big to be lying about like that. I do wish you'd sit up properly.'

She meant I was too fat to loll about in the sun like a white worm. I wondered what she would say if I told her this. I sat up and folded my heavy legs under me and avoided her gaze. 'That's better, dear.'

She was pleased and surprised that I had half done as she wished. To appease me she asked, 'Don't you think my pinks have done wonderfully this year?'

I looked at the flowers and said enthusiastically, 'Yes, wonderfully.'

When she turned away I should lie down again. She turned her attention to Frances. 'Don't make such a noise, dear.'

But her tone was friendly this time. Love welled up in her voice, and though I could not see her face I knew it would be calm and relaxed, not hard and held in check, the lines dragging her mouth down, as when she spoke to me. Frances obediently stopped singing and smiled a charming smile at her mother. 'You've made your face dirty,' she said.

She fingered her own cheek to show better where the dirty mark was. 'Just there,' she said helpfully, and climbing down from the gate came on to the green lawn and, stooping, rubbed my mother's face with her hand. My mother put her arms about her and they knelt as if in ritual, forehead to forehead. I shut my eyes so as not to see them. And while I sat in darkness I could still see them swaying a little on the grass, a small undignified pyramid of love. I felt irritated; Frances after all was not such a very young child. It was affectation to be so trusting. When I opened my eyes it was because Frances was singing: 'Harry-i-et is coming up the road.'

I sat very still, pretending not to have heard, hoping a miracle would take place and Harriet who was coming up the road would dissolve into the warm air and spare me the embarrassment of seeing her.

'Hallo, Harriet, isn't it hot?'

My mother spoke in her coldest voice. Had I been spoken to in this way I would have burst into tears of distress. Cheerfully Harriet said, 'Hallo. I say, your garden looks beautiful.'

She saw me sitting in the porch and waved one hand casually, continuing, 'I believe you must have green fingers.'

She walked along the path and studied the earth, face serious.

'Father has a terrible time with the soil round here, but you seem to have no difficulty.'

My mother struggled bitterly to preserve her displeasure. Her mouth fluttered in distress as she said, 'My pinks have done particularly well this year I must admit.' She capitulated utterly. 'We haven't seen much of you this holiday, dear. You've grown taller I think.'

I made an enormous effort to say something.

'She's not, you know. How high are you, Harriet?'

My mother did not turn her head, and Harriet, pretending not to have heard me, bent low and dug at the soil with her fingers.

'It's the same consistency as ours. I just don't understand it.' She crouched over the flowers, fish-bone-thin vertebrae of her spine showing through her dress, and, humming to herself in a slow sleepy way, touched the plants with her hand, not with the fingers but with the whole palm brushing lightly across the surface of the leaves, as if she were blind. My mother gazed down at her wonderingly. A fluted giggle escaped my lips. In another moment my mother would be down on her knees amongst the pinks. The quick tears came even as I giggled. Their eyes turned to look at me, and I opened my own as wide as possible to stop the tears from falling on to my cheeks, shaming me.

'I was just thinking of something I heard on the wireless,' I explained, seeing them blur and run together in the moisture of my eye.

We had tea on the porch. Mother wanted to sit more respectably in the back garden among the lupins and the roses, but Frances pleaded to be able to have hers in the front.

'It's full of bumblebees in the back,' she argued, screwing up her face desperately, as if already one of the creatures hummed and worried about her head. She was terrified of bees and wasps, and at this time of the year the garden behind the house lay like a golden bowl heaped full of flowers shimmering and quivering with minute fragile life.

So we all had tea in the front as she wished. Mother had a deck-chair. There was no room for more chairs, so we were allowed to sit on cushions at her feet. Frances, a piece of currant bread in one hand, wandered back and forth from porch to gate and gate to porch, to drink from a cup that left her mouth pale and milk-filmed. Harriet and my mother talked intimately about a book they had both read, and did little to draw me into the conversation. I was surprised that my mother had chosen from the library a book such as Harriet would like, and surprised too that my mother did not think it a strange thing for a child of thirteen to understand. Harriet said :

'You see I've read so many books now which just tell a story that I begin more and more to go after style, rather than dramatic content.'

'Really,' said my mother. Her eyes looked at Harriet with wonder and admiration. The beautiful smooth skin of her cheeks and brow, roughened a little by the sun, glowed rosily as she held out her hand for Harriet's cup.

'You see,' the wonder child continued wickedly, 'in this book you had style and content very finely mixed, but I could have done with less.'

'Stuff,' I wanted to shout rudely. It distressed me that Harriet was baiting my mother so. I was pleased to hear in Harriet's voice the slightly flat vowels and nasal intonations of the neighbourhood. It made her a little less perfect, a little more common-seeming. I studied her minutely to find more flaws, this time physical ones. But the bland face with its arched brows and small dry mouth was so dear and familiar to me that I no longer saw it clearly, however much I tried.

Even as I looked at the thin child's body with its bony hips and spine, so oddly at variance with the clever meticulous mind that flourished plump and powerful within, Harriet looked at me and smiled. She seemed to say, 'Yes, you know and I know, but no one else.'

Frances, who was leaning on the gate, suddenly cowered sideways and put her arms up helplessly as if to avoid a blow. A sound as of a cat mewing came from her lips as she spun round to face us, head grotesquely on one side. She screamed once, sharply. Mother ran down the path making small sounds of distress, arms held wide. Frances backed away from her, screaming thinly and uniformly; arms stuck out in front of her as if in supplication, she crouched against the gate, evading the passionate circlet of arms that my mother held out like a garland for her head. It seemed an age before Frances was aware of anything but her pain. Through her own tears my mother asked, 'But what is it, darling . . . tell Mummy what it is.'

It was difficult to distinguish the words through the sharp intakes of breath.

'A thing in my ear . . . in my head.'

'It must have been a wasp,' said Harriet. 'It must have stung her.'

We took her indoors and my mother telephoned the doctor. She sat with Frances on her knee, cradling the shocked child in her arms, till he should come.

Harriet and I went out into the field at the back of the house. I felt I was choking. It had been so sudden, so violent. We climbed the bank that led to the Trail. The Trail was a long mound of earth built to separate the field in half, planted with trees and thorn bushes. On one side were the rows of houses with their ordered unremarkable gardens, on the other the wire netted compounds spread with sand, belonging to the farm. They housed pigs, hens and rabbits. When we were younger, too small to go to the shore, we had struggled along the Trail every evening after tea, making believe that we were escaping across the frontier, leading a line of grateful soldiers. Harriet led the way, and as before I had become aware how small in reality the Norman church was in the blurred woods, so now the trail dwindled and shrank into a trivial line of twisted trees. We came out among the blackberry bushes at the far end of the field and Harriet lay down in the yellow grass and shut her eyes. I sat a little way off and looked for ants in the soil. Poplars swayed elegantly with insect tattered leaves under the high white sky; a blade of grass swung in the breeze and filled the world. Presently Harriet said, 'That was horrible. That was so degrading.'

She sat up and leaned on one elbow to look at me. The park-keeper nearby rode his electric mowing machine over the already prim grass. The noise of the engine was like a bee humming with purpose.

'It's something as tiny and devastating as an insect that we need to humble the Tsar,' Harriet said. She sat up and crossed her legs. On her cheek, where her fist had pressed, was a red mark. It looked like a blow that had been dealt in anger.

'To humble the Tsar,' I repeated stupidly. 'I thought you had forgotten all about that.'

There was a long silence in the field. In the silence there was a warning. It was in the air and the poplars and the earth beneath me, and it was swollen out by the steady insistent note of the grass mower as it turned in a wide circle and rode in our direction. Nearer and nearer it came until I was deafened by the sound of it. And just as it seemed as if I would cry out, the mower wheeled and started back up the park, the noise of its engine receding and dying away, and Harriet, the mark on her face faded now, bent her head on its thin neck and looked at the earth.

'Something really subtle,' she said, 'if you understand me.'

How could I not understand her. I would have given all the power of my too imaginative mind and all the beauty of the fields and woods, not to understand her. And at last I gave in to Harriet, finally and without reservation. I wanted the Tsar to be humiliated, to cower sideways with his bird's head held stiffly in pain and fear, so that I might finish what I had begun, return to school forgetting the summer, and think only of the next holidays that might be as they had always been.

14

THE Tsar and I strolled together under the pine trees. At first when I had met him at the bend of the lane to the sea, he had been sulky with me, withdrawn. There were, it seemed, too many memories in the woods around us for him to be anything but resentful. The blind window in the church nearby, the tadpole pools, dry now, where first we had spoken together, the sand dunes that Harriet had filled with echoes of derision – all served to accentuate his misery and render him inarticulate.

Then it was I had the idea to go right away from our usual paths.

'Let's walk somewhere we don't usually go,' I told him gently, and he straightened his shoulders and said, 'Right you are, but where?'

'Through the Rhododendron Lands and up behind the rifle range.'

For a moment he hesitated. The rifle range was out of bounds to civilians and dangerous, and it might have occurred to him that it was another trap set by Harriet. Then because even walking into a trap was preferable to this feeling of emptiness, he said :

'Good, shall we start?'

Under the trees he told me with difficulty, 'I want you to know I regret the other night more than I can say. It's not a question of shame, it's more a question of shabbiness. And it wasn't the drink.' He faltered and looked at me quickly and away again, moistening his dry lips with his tongue.

I wondered what part of the evening he regretted, the time when he tried to pull down my knickers or when he lay on the floor and cried. I wanted to say he need not feel shabby, that such things happened in the best-regulated families, but it seemed too light-hearted. Instead I said, 'I know how you feel . . . as if something was spoilt.' I turned my face from him and smiled, showing all my teeth. It was quite easy to bring myself to hurt him, he was such a fool.

The smell of beech and pine mingled in the woods. We inhaled its sweetness with every breath we took. It did not seem to matter that every breath I exhaled poured forth poison and evil.

The Tsar said, 'As if something were spoilt . . . I think not. There was nothing to spoil. Harriet saw to that.'

Always Harriet. No matter if he had told me he loved me, it was Harriet who engrossed him.

'When my wife came back,' continued the Tsar, 'she knew you had been in the house. God knows how she knew, but she did. She stood in the dorway and looked at me and she knew. She said, "They've been here they have, those terrible children, they have, haven't they?"' He stumbled and nearly fell into one of the potholes. His voice shook with shock, 'I didn't tell her, but she knew.'

'Why has Mrs Biggs's sister got an idiot child?' I asked.

'Something to do with brain damage at birth,' he said.

'Has it really got a big head?'

'I've never seen it. We're not a close family. The birth went normally to begin with.'

I held my breath because though I knew all about that sort of thing, I'd only read it; no one had ever spoken of it to me before. Long before Harriet and I knew about things I had read in a book the word 'pregnant'. My mother said it meant being very ill and though I knew she was stupid, I still half believed her.

'She was given gas and air to make her sleepy. In the middle of her sleepiness she heard herself singing verse after verse of "There is a Green Hill Far Away". And when she reached the line "O dearly, dearly, has He loved," she began to laugh.' He looked at me to see how I was taking it.

'When did they tell her the baby was funny?' I asked. I felt pale and sick, frightened of something. No wonder the sister of Mrs Biggs laughed when she thought how dearly, dearly had He loved.

'Later on, when they realised the child was hardy enough to survive.'

'Why?' I was shouting. 'Why didn't they kill it?'

'Now, why indeed?' He looked up at the sky above the trees. His eyes were bloodshot as if he had cried too much or smoked too much. He said, 'I don't know why. Some people are born blind, or deaf, or with minds warped in some way. But you can't kill them all . . . you wait for famine or flood or war. After that, you believe in a Divine wisdom.'

'I didn't know you believed in God. I thought for you it was Greece and all those ancient ruins.'

He laughed at me. He stopped walking and felt in his pocket for cigarettes. He stood with hunched shoulders while he lit one, and as he blew out smoke his thin neck reared up like a tortoise emerging from its shell.

I had noticed before that he felt more sure of himself when he smoked. I thought it might be one of the things that hurt Mrs Biggs beyond endurance, goading her to call him weak and in need of discipline. It was a habit that would seem after years without love to epitomise the selfishness she ascribed to him. Just when she felt he was sorry that he had hurt her by his self-preoccupation, and that this once he understood and would make an effort to feel some part of what she suffered, she would turn and find him standing perhaps by the window, his hand already creeping insidiously into his jacket to reach his cigarettes, and she would know again how selfish he was, isolated behind his cloud of smoke.

We walked on and passed the line of warning noticeboards at the edge of the dunes. Rifle shots came spasmodically like twigs breaking underfoot, but the Tsar seemed not to notice, relaxed now, talking charmingly and breathing out smoke into the evening air. The sky that had been infinitely wide and white began to darken; the light squeezed out; everything began to fade. A seagull cried out and the wind dragged its note forlornly across the beach as we dipped and rose like birds among the hillocks of sand. On a sandhill, a red flag on the end of a stick fanned out across the sky, stayed for an instant blood red, rolled slowly in the breeze and blackened.

'It must be getting late,' I shouted.

The Tsar was already climbing the little hill and did not hear. He went on all fours up the face of the dune, his hands reaching out to grasp wildly at the tufts of grass that grew in the sand and whose dry harsh blades were like knives to the touch. I shouted again and he turned, his face small and white, the scanty hair blowing about his ears. 'Come on,' he shouted back. The world was so desolate and darkening that it seemed swept by violence. The sea behind me yawned, a gigantic yawn that never reached its climax. The mouth of the world opened and the rough tongue of the sea licked the shore and tried to suck us down into the depths. Above, the triumphant Tsar held the flag aloft. He shouted something, but it sounded like a moan of protest in the huge land. Firing broke out behind him. I wondered if unwittingly I had outdone Harriet in subtlety, if the ending would be the Tsar shot dead with a red flag for danger clutched in the hand.

'Take care,' I called.

My voice sounded girlish and remote, belonging to Sunday mornings after church when we ran about under the trees and mimicked the Canon, crying, 'Blessed are the meek for they shall inherit the earth.'

I climbed laboriously up to the Tsar. It was lighter here; plainly I could see the row of target boards behind him.

'Let's go down there and rest.'

He pointed below to a small valley between the targets and the dunes. His eyes watched my face for some sign of protest.

'Yes,' I said, and slid downwards into the near darkness. A shot whined somewhere above us. I was glad the Tsar could not see my face or its expression. We lay in the sand and he smoked. It was cold and damp but curiosity kept me there. It was completely dark now, too dark to see my own hands, only the end of the Tsar's cigarette sweeping in an arc from his side to his lips. I thought how I would be careful to shake the sand out of my hair before I saw my parents, how I would wake tomorrow and it would all be over.

'Now,' said the Tsar finally, as if he had been preparing all along for this moment, and flinging his dying cigarette into the night, he turned to me. He sought me in the darkness as if I was a bundle of rags, unwrapping me in layers. I thought of a picture I had seen in a book of an Egyptian king with an arched painted face of repose, and pursed my mouth primly in imitation. Minute grains of sand slid through my hair. The hard collar of his shirt hurt my chin. He did not kiss my mouth, he said nothing. There was no strength in his arms, no pressure of sand beneath me, no swinging meteorite and swift along the orbit of the moon. Pinned there raptureless, a visit to the doctor, nothing more, and a distant uneasy discomfort of mind and body as if both had been caught in a door that had shut too quickly. 'Gerroff,' I wanted to shout, 'Gerroff.' But I did not want to hurt his feelings.

Mrs Biggs, in her sandals and her groping search after love, came alive. She breathed heavily in the darkness, whispering softly, rapidly in my ear, 'He's selfish, he's so selfish. I told you so.' And when the Tsar had completed his own uncomplicated ritual accompanied as it was by low whimpers of distress, I did not know what to do. Harriet I knew would have sworn at him and made him cry, but I could not. The truth was that I was fond of him. He was part of the small group of souls that I was responsible for, who depended on me not to hurt them : my mother, my father, Frances. It did not occur to me till later that the Tsar should feel responsible for me.

'We had better go,' I said as gently as I was able.

He got to his feet and shrugged sand free from his clothes, not speaking. He followed me up the dune and in my mind I knew what he must look like, shambling red-eyed and slack-limbed up the shifting sand.

I was surprised how little discomfort I felt, apart from a kind of interior bruising, and how cheerful I was. I swung my arms vigorously, rejoicing that I was young and not out of condition like he was. I almost ran in the darkness and he stumbled in my wake, breathing harshly. Once he said, 'Stop,' and then, 'Not so fast,' but I went even quicker. It would have been better I thought, with amusement, if he had been shot on the sand dune and avoided all this. It was delicious to be in the position that Harriet alone had enjoyed – to have someone meekly follow wherever I chose to go. I wanted to shout commands, to have the Tsar do tricks to satisfy my vanity. 'Sit up and beg,' I wanted to cry; 'balance on your head.' How often in the past had Harriet with imperious voice and sweetly smiling face, bidden me fasten her shoe-lace in the street. And I, scarce knowing what lay behind the innocent-seeming request, had knelt before her in the road, only to look up in the middle of my task and see her expression of gratified power. Each time she made me kneel to fasten her shoe I expected her to kick me from her, disgusted at my servility.

I no longer cared if we were seen together, the Tsar and I. If Mrs Biggs herself had confronted us on the shore I would have wished her a pleasant good evening and continued on my way. Half-way along the shore we met Perjer, a dim shape at the edge of the water. Seeing him standing there and not knowing who he was I walked slower to allow the Tsar to catch up with me. The Tsar said in a low voice as we drew level, 'Good night,' and Perjer turned and thrust his face close to mine in the darkness.

'Good evening. Calm evening now.'

There was a moment of silence as if both men could not make up their minds.

'It is Mr Biggs, isn't it?'

'We've been miles along the shore, Mr Perjer. It's so beautiful at this time of the evening.'

Perjer said nothing to this. He moved closer to the Tsar. 'I haven't seen you and your good lady in a long time. Keeping well, is she?'

It seemed comical to hear Mrs Biggs referred to as a good lady.

'Oh yes, well enough, thank you . . . you all right?'

The Tsar had tried to be formal but Perjer was a lost soul like himself. I sensed his face relaxed in the darkness. He said almost jovially:

'Still on the water wagon?'

Perjer grunted. 'Now and then,' he said, and grunted again.

The conversation seemed ended. The Tsar jerked my arm with his elbow and I cleared my throat in preparation for a polite farewell.

He said with exasperation: 'Damn, I've run out of matches – got a light, Perjer?'

'In my hut.' He moved away and called into the wind, 'Mind how you go! Careful of the wire!'

They disappeared into the blackness. Far out to sea squares of light twinkled beneath the starless sky. The wind blew steadily above the dull breathing of the sea, as it covered the sand. The Tsar called remotely, 'Come on, what's the matter?'

I walked slowly in the direction of the sound, burying my hands deep in the pockets of my coat.

The hut was below a sandhill that hung out over it forming a second roof. Coming into the light, I blinked my eyes and heard the hum of the paraffin lamp swinging from a hook in the ceiling. There was a wood fire and a black kettle without a lid, in the embers. Perjer's dog raised a tired head from the sand-covered floor and lay flat again. The Tsar went and sat with his back to the far wall, stretching his legs out in front of him. He dug at the dog's ribs with his foot and sank his head lower on to his chest. I was annoyed that the Tsar was so evidently at home, that he had been here before.

There was an upturned box behind the door, so I sat on that and kept watching Perjer. There was nothing of him in the black clothes that hung in folds on his body. The hands and wrists seemed without arms, the neck waved stemlike to support his oval head. Only the full mouth in the dark face was alive, pouting and grimacing continually. He tore a strip from a newspaper on the floor, and lighting it at the fire held it out to the Tsar who waited cigarette in hand. No one spoke in the hut; sand slithered down from somewhere above us, and a little of it poured in a fine stream through a crack in the roof. It fell on the dog's head, who moved in his sleep and a spasm shook his ears free of it.

Perjer got more wood from a pile in the corner of the hut, and removing the black kettle from the embers and placing it with a neat house-proud precision on a rough shelf above the door, he returned and kicked the wood into place and rubbed his hands together.

The Tsar said, 'It's not too warm is it?' His eyes took in the worn black suit. 'I expect that's wearing a bit thin now.'

It sounded personal and in my ignorance I feared Perjer would be offended.

'I wore it on my wedding day,' said the Tsar.

He looked at me and away again. Perjer squatted by the dog; placing his palms on his knees, he looked down contemplatively at the black cloth across his breast.

'We all come to it,' he said, as if comforting a child.

Perjer cradled the dog's paw in his. 'I sat on the wall outside and wished you luck. The Canon tried to get rid of me.'

'Yes, so he did.'

The two men smiled at the recollection and gazed into the fire.

Perjer had been there that day too. Mrs Biggs in her bridal gown, the Canon dropping crumbs from his baby mouth. There on the floor of the hut sat Perjer in the wedding suit the Tsar had worn thirty years ago.

'It was a grand day for it,' said Perjer.

Going home I was silent. The Tsar told me that Perjer was the son of a doctor in London. 'He started out to be a lawyer but he never took his finals. Upset the old man. No staying power at all . . . he just wasn't interested. He said he was born tired.'

'Lazy sod.'

'Quite.'

The lamps were lit in the lane. The windows in the church shone gold; the Canon's sister whom nobody loved was playing the organ. Like the broken window I too had been violated. As Perjer had said this evening . . . we all come to it in the end.

15

THERE were but two weeks left of the holidays. As before at school I had counted the days to the end of term, willing the hours to pass quicker, so now I waited for summer to finish. Shadows of fatigue darkened my face though I went to bed early and slept late each morning. My mother said twice I looked poorly and hoped I was not going to be ill.

I tried to talk to Harriet but there was a barrier between us. She did not mention the diary and we were not allowed out at night. It would have been nice to mention casually that I had been inside Perjer's hut, that he was the son of a doctor in London. And but for Harriet's mother it could have ended then, it need not have gone further.

Harriet was sitting at the kitchen table writing her nature diary. The little woman and I sat twined in cosy intimacy together winding wool.

She said, 'I met Mrs Biggs this morning on her way to the station. Her sister's child has been taken to hospital.'

She looked up, suddenly aware of whom she spoke. I kept my arms held wide and looked at the wool strung across them as if they were strands of gold. Harriet said nothing. I let the silence develop. Then I said, 'What a shame,' and, moving my arms from side to side, 'Why don't they invent a machine to do all this?'

Relieved, the little woman continued winding her ball of wool. The small head bent low was vulnerable. For no reason I thought how easy it would be to crush the skull beneath the

soft hair. All the time I was really thinking of Mrs Biggs, looking at the little woman's feet half expecting to see the square
brown sandals planted firmly on the grey carpet. I knew
Harriet was watching me and I felt afraid. She said in a bright
exultant voice :

'What a bit of luck! I say, little woman, how do you spell
fauna?' It was our old strategy, evolved to cheat the adults at
their own game. The first sentence was for me, the second a
blind to cover the real message. I waited. When the Little
Woman had spelt the word, Harriet said, 'I never expected
that . . . Thank you.'

'We must go there as soon as possible . . . I need another
leaf for my collection.'

If she had said, 'scalp' it would have been more appropriate.

'No, no we can't.' I heard my voice incredulously.

Surprised, the Little Woman stared at me, a frown pucker-
ing her forehead. Harriet pushed her chair back noisily behind
me and came over to her mother.

'Do you like my drawing?'

She sat on the arm of the chair and put an arm round her
mother's shoulders. She looked at me as she said, 'It's a little
uncontrolled, isn't it?'

Her mother said delightedly, 'It's a lovely drawing, darling
. . . and your writing is so much better.'

I sat holding the wool in my hands and looked down at the
floor. 'Very well,' I said, 'but this is the last time.'

I did not mind if her mother was puzzled, it was all one
now. 'Then that's settled. We'll go tomorrow.'

Harriet bent and kissed her mother on the cheek with
fondness. She stood up yawning with satisfaction, stretching her arms high above her head, her eyes closed against her
thoughts.

As before, we met in the lane; but this time nothing was said
about arriving separately at the house of the Tsar. Nor did we
pause in Timothy Street, for fear people should see which way
we went. It was dark when we opened the high gate. It was a

pitifully short path to the front door and the holly bush beside the porch. Some of the light from the lamp in the street spilled through the hedge and lay on the dark lawn.

I told myself, as I lifted the heavy knocker to summon the Tsar, that I should remember all my life the smell of the paint that had blistered in the sun, the sound of Harriet breathing in the blackness, the dry rustle of the coarse hair-mat beneath our feet, as if we stood on fallen leaves.

The Tsar stood as if at the end of a long tunnel, a small figure with hands outstretched.

'Well, invite us in,' said Harriet.

The face of the Tsar was old. He smiled hectically, waggling a reproving finger.

'Naughty, naughty. You shouldn't have come.'

'Well, we have,' she said.

'I could say it's a great pleasure, a deep pleasure. I could indeed say that.' He swayed a little on his feet.

Harriet fell silent. She had not anticipated that he would be drunk. For myself our meeting was mist bound after a lapse of eternity.

Last holidays I had seen Papa, the husband of Dodie, after a period of several months. He was so old all at once, standing in his garden, tottering over the lawn when I called his name. 'Papa,' I had said, 'it's me, don't you remember?'

Behind the hedge he peered at me, holding on to his walking cane, the breeze moving his white hair. A handsome face, still, thick waves of hair on his temples. A long while ago we had been the best of friends – Harriet and Dodie and Papa and I – sharing little jokes, sitting in his garden waiting for the strawberries to ripen, the plums to fall.

So gallant, Papa, in his blazer and boater among the flowers. He stood there, ill and almost blind, and I too sure facing him, watching his groping expression in the sunlight as he fought to thrust aside the years' corrosion and recognise my voice, eyes clouded like milk spilt.

Looking at the Tsar I felt now that he, unlike Papa, was thrusting life away from him with all his power, pushing back-

ward all that might yet keep him nearly young. I said quickly,
'We came to say good-bye. We go back to school at the end
of the week, there's no more time.'

'Ah now, that's a blow.'

The Tsar began to laugh immoderately. He shrugged his
shoulders in a spasm of mirth and tapped the grandfather
clock on its glass middle.

'No more time left,' he recited lovingly, and a deep boom
of protest came from the clock as he leaned heavily against it.
Harriet opened the door into the front-room.

'I'm tired,' she said and walked in. Beyond the doorway I
could see the sofa glimpsed through the window an age ago.
As we stood in the hall with the shrivelled Tsar, it assumed its
proper importance, no longer an altar of sacrifice on which
he had lain, but a comfortable piece of furniture, its design
repeated and echoed in a hundred other rooms in a hundred
other houses. I followed Harriet and sat deliberately on the
sofa. Harriet began to enjoy herself. She hugged her knees
with enjoyment so that the two lank ropes of her hair touched
gently the faded carpet.

'Hark at him,' she said with mock severity as the Tsar
struck at the grandfather clock in the hall. She rolled her eyes
comically as the Tsar half sang, half shouted, 'Ding-Dong,
Ding-Dong.'

'He's mad drunk, that's what he is,' I whispered. 'Stark
raving drunk.'

I leaned backwards on the sofa to see the Tsar laboriously
winding the aged clock.

'Trying to make more time,' he shouted, and broke into
laughter. We laughed too, though it was sad what he said. He
came sideways into the room and shut the door with elegance,
pivoting round on his toes to face us with one hand raised in
blessing.

'So be it,' he said gently to Harriet and walked to the small
table with the bottles stacked on it.

'Is the child very ill?' asked Harriet sitting bolt upright on
one of the chairs by the hearth.

'The child? . . . Oh did she say that?' He poured liquid into a glass and held it up to the light.

'She's gone for a rest. That's what she said. She said I was making her ill. That's what she said.' His voice lifted the last words as if he was reciting a poem.

'It's as good as a play,' said Harriet eyeing him with delight. 'The stage husband deserted by his wife steadily drinking himself into oblivion. The part's made for you.' She curled herself deeper into the massive armchair and looked thoughtful.

'But what are we?' she asked the Tsar.

'Ah now, that's more difficult.' He propped himself against the mantelpiece and pointed the toe of his shoe upwards. 'Angels of light,' he said giving Harriet a sly glance, 'come to show me a way out of it all.'

Delighted with each other's wit they laughed together. It became clearer in my mind. What I had known in the hut on the shore had not been false. Harriet, who had schemed and planned the summer long for this, and who finally believed there was not enough time, could not realise she no longer controlled events. Every breath we took spun the wheel faster and faster, and neither she nor I nor God could stop it. Had I believed God would, I might have prayed, but this too Harriet had perhaps foreseen, for how many times over the years had she taught me that God was powerless without innocence?

Harriet said, 'This place needs brightening up, Tsar. Let's rearrange the furniture.'

She stood and surveyed the room.

'Now this would look much better here.' She seized the armchair with strong hands and pulled it into the centre of the room. 'There.' Head tilted on her thin neck so that the lamplight fell full on to her smooth pale face, she looked at the room. The Tsar stared stupidly at the large armchair in its unfamiliar place.

'It won't do, you know,' he said finally, and moved on precise feet to rescue the chair, but Harriet was already moving swiftly about the room like an uneasy whirlwind, dragging the table from its accustomed place under the window, so that it reared out into the already cluttered room.

The Tsar let go his hold of the isolated chair and tried to push the table into place, but it was too heavy for him and he sprawled breathlessly against it, watching Harriet with disbelief. She, standing on tiptoe, stretched up a violating arm and snatched the statue with its exposed breast from its niche on the sideboard. Holding it aloft she faced him triumphantly.

'This,' she cried, 'ought by rights to be on a raised dais so that Mrs Biggs can pray to the vulgar thing.'

The minute sword brandished in the figure's hand tilted slightly and cast a huge shadow across the curtains.

'No, no, put it down.' The Tsar giggled in a weak fashion and placed his hand on his heart. 'You'll break it . . . Take care.'

He seemed to slip downwards into his neat city clothes, so that they hung on his thin body and fluttered as he moved towards her. 'Put it down,' he repeated in a high fluted voice without control. Harriet darted to the mantelpiece and stood the statue directly in the middle. It leered at the room, its red-tipped breast pointing upwards, its sword rakishly spearing the blue lupins that lolled in their cream vase.

'That's better,' she cried. 'Now Mrs Biggs can get down on her knees to it.'

I kept my eyes fixed on the Tsar so that I should see the exact moment at which he broke under the strain. His face as he looked at the disordered room was almost hopeful. It was as if by changing the position of the furniture Harriet had minutely struck at his life with Mrs Biggs. Each new arrangement of a familiar object blurred and unfocused the years and moments of their existence together, so that he felt in this new catastrophe that the memory of Mrs Biggs was being edged slowly, little by little, out of the room. He wanted to complete the dismissal. He turned to the Welsh dresser and took down the blue and gold plates one by one from their places. His hands moved so clumsily and so eagerly that one fell from his grasp and dropped to the carpet. It did not break but lay reproachfully face down at his feet. All the time I sat upright on the blue sofa, while Harriet and he moved like birds of prey around the stricken room.

Harriet found a match and lit the virgin candles in their brass holders on either side of the hearth. She turned off the electric light and, as the wax melted and the wicks burned, the room was nearly beautiful. Mrs Biggs, had she returned, might have been pleased with the improvements. She might have appreciated the soft leaping shadows on the dull cream walls.

Back and forth in the candlelight the Tsar and Harriet went their destructive way. Now, I told myself, now. Surely she must come back now. And as I said it, the Tsar lifted his foot and kicked at the glass dial of the radio. Harriet, appalled, looked at the wrecked instrument and said slowly, as if returning from a long journey through dangerous places. 'That was stupid . . . You shouldn't have done it.' The face she turned to me was bewildered.

'Let's go home now,' she said, and the childish mouth remained open in fear.

The Tsar stood in the expensive glass, swaying on his feet.

'Why, why?' his voice was accusing. 'You wanted me to do it. You did, didn't you?'

Harriet stood motionless, defenceless in the centre of the room, her mouth quivering.

'Oh come now,' the Tsar spoke to her tenderly, stretching out a hand to her with beguilement, 'I thought it would be a gesture after your own heart.' He looked wonderingly round the shadowed room, taking strength from the new unfamiliarity, and said with gaiety, 'Let's enjoy ourselves while we can. Let's all have a cigarette.'

He patted his pocket hopefully and felt with eager fingers for his case. Harriet said nothing, keeping her eyes fixed on him as one hypnotised by something terrible.

'I'll have to run out and get some.'

He showed us his empty cigarette case with despair. 'Can't possibly be without a cigarette.'

146

He waited as if half expecting Harriet would stop him, and then seeing she only watched him, he moved gladly to the door.

'I won't be long. Just you sit back and enjoy the décor.'

We heard him go down the hall and out of the door. His footsteps went softly down the path, the gate creaked as he opened it and left us alone in the house.

I wondered if the Tsar would ever return in our lifetime. I would have liked to tell Harriet this but her face was so white and mute I left her to her own thoughts. She stood uneasily in the middle of the room not knowing what to do, then because there was nowhere to go sat down on the sofa beside me. In the candlelight the tables and chairs jostled for position; the figure on the mantelshelf flickered and thrust its tiny sword deeper into the flowers. Harriet said, 'He shouldn't have done that.'

She looked fearfully at the broken glass that lapped the carpet.

'It was stupid.'

I could not agree, so I kept silent.

'What's the matter with you?' Her voice was petulant.

'Nothing.' I enjoyed my calmness, my ability to puzzle Harriet, above all the knowledge that she was frightened. She sat up and caught hold of my arm fiercely.

'Why are you so calm all of a sudden . . . tell me?' She pinched my flesh viciously so that I squirmed. Go on, tell me.'

'Nothing. I just don't mind any more.'

Harriet let go of my arm and lay back defeated. The candle nearest the window lurched in its holder and dripped grease on to the carpet, a round globe of wax among the shattered glass. Kindly, I told her: 'You see, dear, we've done what you wanted. We've humbled him like you said.'

Slowly she turned her face to me, the eyes widening, 'What do you mean?'

I almost hesitated but there did not seem any reason now why I should not tell her.

'Well, it happened . . . the other night on the shore. I mean he . . . he . . .' I could not say it.

'He had you?'

Her voice was weak with incredulity. She watched my mouth for a denial, and seeing none came, flung herself back against the arm of the sofa, looking at me as if she had not known me before. Then as the full realisation struck her: 'My God, he had you!'

She stood up and stared wildly round the lunatic room. My mouth twitched in the beginnings of a smile because she embarrassed me. I dug my teeth into my lip in an act of suppression. The phrase she used was comical, it reminded me too much of the sentences we had written with infinite labour in the diary.

I said, 'But I thought that's what you meant me to do. You said we had to bring it to a conclusion. You said so.'

'I didn't say to do that, I never – '

'You said humble him.'

'I never said to do that.' Her shoulders jerked in a spasm of distress. 'Why do a thing like that? We're not ready. You had no right.'

'I don't know what you are fussing about. It was nothing really. I hardly noticed. Just a bit like going to the dentist. Not even as bad.'

I thought she was going to hit me. Instead she spun round and ran from the room. I was left sitting on the blue sofa with the candles burning on the walls. I really couldn't see what she was so angry about. Stifled by a desire to laugh I walked to the door and called her name. I thought for one moment she was not in the house and then in the darkness I heard her whisper, 'She's come back . . . it's Mrs Biggs.'

In the night the dull capable footsteps came up the path. There was nowhere to go, nowhere to hide; my heart beat so loudly I was afraid Mrs Biggs must hear it. I stood beside Harriet behind the door and she pressed against me and clenched my hand reassuringly. I struggled to preserve my independence as Mrs Biggs stood in the porch, battled my will against Harriet's, and as the key fitted in the lock and the wife of the Tsar leaned her weight against the door, Harriet pushed something into my hand.

'Hit her,' she said softly, 'hit her.'

The door opened inward and I stepped out into the centre of the hall raising my arm high above my head. She was huge and menacing in the porch and I meant to push her down the steps so that Harriet and I might run away. When I hit her she swayed on her feet, unaccountably facing the dark garden, and did not fall. I struck at her again with desperation and boldness because she could not see my face, and when she fell softly away from me and drifted into the darkness like some great leaf, the Tsar was standing in the open gateway looking at me.

I could not move, I could not lower my arm. Harriet switched the hall light on behind me and I felt the night air sweeping over the plot of grass to cool my face. I wept inside and loved my mother and my father with all my being, but I could not move.

The Tsar came along the path slowly as if he were very tired. I wanted him to hurry so that I might be released from my inertia and he could tell me that nothing after all was wrong. I hoped Mrs Biggs would stay with her face on the steps till Harriet and I had run home. I could not bear the weight of the stick in my hand and I hoped too that the Tsar would take it from me and put it back in its stand behind the door with Mrs Biggs's red and green umbrella.

'Go inside,' the Tsar said. 'Go inside and don't come out.'

I was frightened but I did what he told me. I had done something wrong and he and Mrs Biggs united would talk to me severely. This time for sure Mrs Biggs would come and visit my mother. I was glad they would all be angry with me now because I had felt so strangly vindictive when I struck at Mrs Biggs; I should be punished and purged, could kiss Harriet on the cheek and return to school never more to think of the Tsar and this dreadful summer. Harriet had blown out the candles and put on the electric light, reducing the room to shabby disorder. I was surprised she just stood there and did not rush frantically putting the furniture to rights so that Mrs Biggs would not be further shocked.

'I didn't hit her very hard, Harriet. I only meant to push her.'

Harriet said 'Yes' absently and rubbed at her cheek.

'What if she has to go to hospital?' With fear beginning I looked at her for reassurance.

'She won't.'

The front door closed loudly and the Tsar came into the room. He stood in the doorway looking at the glass on the carpet and felt in his pocket for cigarettes. He hunched his shoulders and thrust his jaw forward so that I could see the faint perspiration on his face when the match flared up. The smoke from his cigarette wreathed his head familiarly, clouding the sparse hair. Harriet at the mantelshelf raised her hand and brushed the lupins with her palm, shaking the loaded stems gently. 'She's dead,' said the Tsar.

Someone was crying, sobbing as if their heart would break, making ugly sounds in the otherwise silent room. My face puckered up, though inside I was calm. My father was saying I had done it now, I had really done it this time, and I was arguing with him rationally, telling him that Mr Biggs did rude things to me in the sandhills, that it was not my fault, I had been corrupted. More sinned against than sinning. I was shouting but he would not listen and Mrs Biggs was straddling over me, shaking me furiously in giant hands, stamping on my feet with her great sandals and I was telling her to get off, get off me you big fat sow, but I could not get my breath and my tongue would not shape the words. Then she shook me so violently the room slid headlong past me and receded. Harriet was pushing the small of my back with a rough hand, forcing my head between my knees and when I sat up I was on the blue sofa. The Tsar was not in the room. There was a stale smell of sickness all over me; my hair was sticky.

I could not make out what Harriet was telling me. Something about time and the fact that the Tsar had got his cigarettes from the slot machine at the station.

'Nobody saw him at the station; he says it was completely deserted.' She spoke urgently into my ear, her warm breath fanning my cheek. 'And nobody saw him in the street either, he's sure of it.'

In just a few days I could go back to school. In just a few days. Today my father would have bought the train ticket. It would be lying on the hall table when I went in. I held on to the thought of the train ticket while Harriet's voice went on and on . . .

'Nobody saw us come here. We'll go out through the back garden and along the ditch. We'll come quickly up the side lane into the street again and I will scream. Then we will run all the way to my house and when they ask us what is wrong we'll say we saw the Tsar hit Mrs Biggs.'

She leant over me powerfully and took me by the shoulders. 'We'll say we saw the Tsar hit Mrs Biggs . . . do you hear?'

I did love Harriet then. She was so wise, so good, so sweetly clever and able to cope with the situation. I would say we saw Mrs Biggs fall down the steps, and the Tsar behind her with a stick in his hand.

'Yes, Harriet, I'll say that.'

Now that Mrs Biggs was truly dead I would do whatever Harriet wanted. I would never doubt her again but acknowledge she was more beautiful than me.

She stood up and looked quickly at the room. She searched in the pocket of her dress for her handkerchief and began to wipe the mantelpiece. The Tsar came into the room and closed the door behind him. He watched Harriet thoughtfully for a moment and then said:

'What are you doing?'

I was glad he asked her that because I wanted to know too.

'There'll be fingerprints,' said Harriet, 'and we don't want that. If we're thorough no one will guess we've been here.'

She took down the statue from above the fireplace and wiped it carefully.

'I see.'

There was a long silence while Harriet finished what she had to do. She even rubbed the door knob and the edge of the table.

'Now we'll go,' she said with authority. She eyed him carefully to see if he was equal to the situation, and having satisfied herself, continued :

'You must wait at least an hour for us to get home and tell our story.'

I waited fearfully for the Tsar to ask what our story was, but he stood by the window and said nothing.

'Then you must phone the police and tell them Mrs Biggs is dead. Do you understand?'

The old man nodded his head and fingered the material of the curtain.

'It's important you wait that hour. You do see that, don't you?'

'Quite.'

'Good.' She looked at me and made a slight upward gesture with her hand. I stood up obediently and followed her out of the room.

She closed the door behind me and leaned against it, her eyes searching the hall. 'The stick,' she said, but not to me.

It was in its stand along with the red umbrella with green stripes. She lifted it out carefully and wiped at it with the grey lining of her coat.

Above the clock was a shelf with a blue plate. There was one like it at home. Outside in the porch Mrs Biggs slept on. The clock ticked on.

Then we walked out of the back door into the garden.